ROSES ARE DEAD

Jen has broken free of a stifling relationship and is celebrating life afresh, enjoying her independence in a new flat — until strange gifts start to arrive. With Valentine's Day approaching, the mystery of who is sending them disturbs her. She fears it could be Harris, her ex; but when things turn sinister, she doesn't know who to trust: her ex, her neighbour, Sergeant Aidan Lee or just herself. When Jen needs help, who will come?

VALERIE HOLMES

ROSES ARE DEAD

Complete and Unabridged

LINFORD
Leicester

First published in Great Britain in 2013

First Linford Edition
published 2014

A catalogue record for this book is available
from the British Library.

ISBN 978–1–4448–1827–7

Published by
F. A. Thorpe (Publishing)
Anstey, Leicestershire

Set by Words & Graphics Ltd.
Anstey, Leicestershire
Printed and bound in Great Britain by
T. J. International Ltd., Padstow, Cornwall

This book is printed on acid-free paper

1

Patience is running out. I was here on time. Where are you?

Little Miss Perfect is always on time. Staring across through a misty window, deliberately obscuring the view in — not the view out. I wait. Come on . . . time waits for no man — or woman. You should know that. Ten minutes I've been here and still no sign. Come on! Ah, at last . . .

Monday 11th February 2013:

Target: Jennifer Brightman

Crime: Betrayal.

Observations: leaves apartment at 7.35a.m. precisely, later than expected for one usually so punctual. Dressed practically/smart. Unlocks new Mini Cooper — Blood-red — How appropriate! Throws heavy bag on back seat. Drives off. Manner: confident. No time to strike now. Everyone can change and you will as you have made me. Let the sentence begin . . .

★   ★   ★

Jen reversed out of her drive as she did every Monday morning, punctual and prepared for the week ahead, but this time, instead of feeling dreary, she glanced back at the door of her new ground floor apartment and smiled, acknowledging Mr Marshall's presence in the garden of his 1930's semi-detached.

Always an early riser, her neighbour was surveying the world from his garden, admiring his neat borders, with his mug of hot tea in hand. Although he was now retired, widowed in fact, his day was his own and so he could sleep in at will, but he never seemed to. Old habits, Jen presumed, died hard.

She sped away, feeling exhilarated and in control of her own life. It was a new sensation inspired by the desire to be free and, for once, owning the surroundings in which to enjoy it — her lovely apartment, all of one week old.

She drove past the car park entrance opposite, noticing the parked police car in the small car park. There would only be a few people wandering around in it at this hour, normally with their dogs, it was a bit early for the police to be present. If there was trouble in there it was on a Friday or Saturday night.

She slowed down as a man walked his Airedale across the road ahead. One day she might buy a dog — a spaniel perhaps, soft and loyal — but not just yet. Jen still had too much to accomplish on her 'to do' list of musts before she reached the age of thirty in just under a year's time. Dogs were like children that never grew up, when it came to dependency that is, and Jen had plans which meant she needed to be free.

This morning Jen was ready to guide the next generation in the very basics of essential skills at the beginning of their life's journey. She smiled at the grand thought. Well, teaching them which way up to hang their coats on their own peg was a start.

Her life, now, was looking up, or at least that was how it felt; she was experiencing a rebirth, a new phase, a beginning of her journey into the next exciting phase of her life, one where she could breathe deeply and enjoy her own privacy.

* * *

Twenty minutes later she had pulled off the busy dual carriageway north of Ebton, which seemed to separate the coastal town from the moor roads, and turned left into a cul-de-sac through some old council housing. She stopped at the gates momentarily, before entering the car park of the school, just in case any of the children had escaped and run back into the parking area.

Sheila arrived at South Hallenton Primary just a few minutes after Jen.

'Morning!' she said brightly.

Her voice made Jen look up from her table, noting that her friend and teaching assistant's normal Monday morning blues seemed to have lifted today. Instead of her half-hearted yawn, she was smiling brightly.

'Tell me, what has caused that lively note in your voice — and was that a detectable bounce in your step that I observed as you came in? It can't be a lottery win or you wouldn't be here, would you?' Jen grinned at the other woman's happy face.

Life, Jen thought, had never been so good, not for a long time — and it appeared that she was not the only one who was feeling this way.

'Who would? No, not a lottery win. Shame, though, that would really solve a lot of problems. It's more a case of a love rekindled.' Sheila put up her hand to silence and protest from Jen. 'No, my curious friend, it is so much more romantic than that.' She gave a cheeky knowing look in Jen's direction.

'You are married, Mrs, so why are

you speaking of romance?' She imitated Sheila's intonation as she spoke. 'And at this hour on a Monday morning, too.' She feigned a shocked expression. 'Tell me — wherever did you two spend the weekend?'

Jen had moved away from her own table, deciding to busy herself with a distraction. She began stacking paper near the paint corner, ready for the 'fun' to begin with twenty-nine five year olds and under. She smiled tentatively as she glanced back at her friend, not wanting to make eye contact with her, as she began forcing the unwelcome images of Kevin, Sheila's husband, from her mind. This was not a conversation she wanted to be a part of.

Jen tucked one of her wayward auburn locks behind her ear as she bent over, wishing she had decided to fasten her shoulder-length hair up out of the way before she had left. Sheila did not have those kinds of hair issues, wearing it short and perpetually dyed blonde.

'At home, nothing special there, just

the usual stuff . . . except that I accidently stumbled on a very lovely surprise and I'm absolutely thrilled by it.'

Sheila dropped her bag onto a chair and hung up her coat before quickly drinking the mug of coffee that was waiting for her by the classroom microwave.

'What surprise would that be?' Jen asked, out of politeness, not wanting to spoil her friend's moment of revelation, yet not sure she wanted to know any more details.

'Thursday's, silly. You know, Valentine's Day! Doh!' She looked skyward. 'Kevin's terrible at keeping anything a secret, but this time I knew he was trying to and so I just happened to be putting his clothes away when I opened his drawer and . . . ' She stopped and covered her mouth with her hand, regret written across her face.

Jen knew what was coming and wished that her life had not been so open to her workplace friends. It made some situations awkward, if not downright difficult. This time, though, her expression had been misunderstood. Sheila was lovely, but Jen knew to her cost that Kevin was actually very good at keeping some secrets.

Jen really could have done better for herself, but love, as she also knew to her cost, was frequently blind and deaf.

'I'm sorry, Jen. I didn't think . . . ' Sheila looked around the room distractedly.

Jen busied herself inside the painting corner, preparing the sponges and laying out newspaper over the painting table and surrounding floor. Really Sheila should have already done this, but Jen was in a good mood so she let Sheila continue chatting as she organised the activity for the morning session.

'You don't need to be sorry. I'm well over Harris and I have my own flat now. I'm happily single and free. Sheila, don't look like that, believe me I really am happy — life has never been so good. Go on then, tell me what you found in his drawer. Share the goss.'

Sheila instantly relaxed.

'Well you tell me what you think about this then . . . a pair of ruby drop earrings. So gorgeous, they're just like little hearts, held in place with twisted gold. Best ever! Usually, I get chocolates and a card, if I'm lucky.'

She chuckled and added, 'Once you have kids things slip a bit, I guess.'

She was smiling, but Jen saw a fleeting glimpse of regret flash across her friend's eyes. She also noted that her eyes had given Jen a quick once over, but Jen was a size 12, had not had two children and was quite fit, whereas Sheila was a much stockier build. Jen had no experience of having a family, so could not really comment she supposed, but she did not believe that 'slipping' was compulsory.

'Very nice, they sound lovely. You're going to have to work hard at looking genuinely surprised when he gives them to you, though. So what have you got for him?' Jen asked, and saw her friend's face turn pale.

The bell rang out for the start of the first period.

'Good point,' Sheila replied, as their busy day began. 'Looks like I'll be going shopping after school.' She smiled. 'I'd better get the grey cells working to think of something suitably surprising in exchange for his surprise. I can't compete with a gift like that, not on my salary.'

Sheila paused then winked at Jen. 'You really should be back on the chase, Jen. You're young and time is slipping by . . . '

'Oh, look, talking of time slipping by, here they come . . . ' Jen nodded to the children as the first few arrived at the door to their part of the lower school; she stood up to greet some mums and walked off.

Today she was smiling, she felt happy and nothing was going to change that, not even the mention of her lack of love life — or of Kevin.

* ★ ★ ★

Monday was its usual mixture of chaos around the carefully planned out structure of the day's intended activities.

By 3p.m. Jen was left with just Michelle, the most mature and oldest pupil in the class. The girl was used to being with her gran and seemed to like keeping the company of adults more than the other children. She was her usual challenging self: silent and moody one minute, chatty and inquisitive the next. However, she had only joined the school in the New Year so she was still finding her place among an established class.

The other children had been collected, but Michelle was still waiting there.

'No sign of Gran yet?' Sheila asked her.

Michelle looked a little uneasy, as if she was going to be told off, and shook her head, her eyes still fixed on Jen rather than looking out for her grand-mother coming or at Sheila.

'Are you staying with Gran tonight?' Sheila persisted. She had asked her question casually, but Jen knew that she was wondering why the girl's mother never seemed to show up.

Michelle had been registered at the school by her mother — no mention of the father — but the only person the staff had seen so far was Michelle's grandmother picking her up. She always waited on the path for Michelle to come out to her.

Jen tried to encourage the girl to spend more time with her peers and less mimicking the adults. She seemed mature beyond her years in speech and observation, but not perhaps in her understanding.

'Do you ever play in the park, miss?' Michelle asked Jen quite unexpectedly.

Jen was always surprised by the girl's comments. She required more patience as her questions could be quite direct and it also meant that if her intelligence was not challenged she would often act as if she was bored.

'No, Michelle. I don't play in the park, but I sometimes walk through it to see the squirrels.' Jen looked out of the window for Michelle's grandmother.

Really, if this happened too often she would have to speak to her about collecting Michelle on time.

Michelle stood beside her, almost mimicking Jen's stance as she looked out.

'It's not safe to do that, Miss Brightman. Gran says that — oh, here she is now . . . Bye!'

She ran for the door. Jen watched her go before heading back to the classroom to put the chaos back into order before attending the planning meeting in the staffroom. It was a shame, she thought, how a child was not allowed to play in a beautiful park and enjoy the open air.

'Sign of the times,' she muttered to herself. Jen lived opposite a park, with a lovely lake in its centre, where squirrels and ducks abounded and children frequently played.

Jen stared for a moment at the car park outside, devoid of parents and children. Had Michelle meant her park, or had it just been one more of the girl's throwaway questions? She shook her head and chastised herself for her fanciful thoughts. After all, how would the child know she lived opposite a park?

Jen gave a quick side-long glance at the school clock.

'Duty calls!' she said, and smiled as she went to her meeting. One last event of the day and then she could return to her lovely new home.

* * *

Two hours later she parked her Mini outside the apartment, dragged out her bag from the car, thinking she would need a postman's trolley soon if the paperwork blossomed further, and thought about having a nice glass of

Merlot in her new kitchen while making dinner, but as she saw the mailbox she paused.

With her free hand she turned the door key, which released the mail box flap. It fell open as usual, but Jen had to jump back a step as a mass of red rose petals cascaded onto the ground at her feet.

'What the . . . ?' Jen exclaimed, staring at them as well as those left in the box, and then returned her attention to the scattered profusion of red debris littering the ground. They were beautiful — fresh, yet so unexpected. Who had left them?

Looking left and right, there was no sign of anyone watching her from the park or along the road; only parked cars and a van on the road opposite. True, there were people and children in the park, but they all seemed too busy playing or going about their business to notice her.

Jen stared into the box to see if there was a note to explain why they were there — something to tell her what this prank was all about. The letter on the floor of the mailbox had no petals underneath it.

'After the post then,' Jen muttered to herself, then glanced to see if Mr Marshall was in his bay window — on lookout, as she called it. There was no sign of him. Her post usually arrived late in the afternoon. Mr Marshall had informed her of this as he did most things.

'Who would play such a stunt?' she asked herself out loud, as if the answer would be supplied by the gentle breeze which was beginning to stir the mass of red petals, swirling them around her ankles. Jen could not help but admire this spectacle realising they would not have been cheap, they were so delicate and lovely, a truly vibrant red.

'Who buys fresh rose petals on their own?'

Once her initial surprise had worn off, Jen bent down to feel their velvety beauty. Whoever had placed them there had done so carefully so as not to crush the petals as they passed through the opening.

With her bag placed safely in her kitchen, Jen fetched a bowl from inside the flat and collected her unexpected gift up from the ground before it was blown away and wasted.

'Sheila? Must be.' The words escaped her lips as if voicing it gave the thought credibility.

Sheila had been talking about Valentine's Day only that morning — she was such a romantic fool! She must have swung around by the florist's on The Parade, a local line of shops on the edge of town, when she went shopping, and played such a daft prank to try to bolster Jen's ego.

Jen smiled. There was no need for such a lavish and foolish gesture — and it was not even Valentine's Day yet.

Jen was free and single and that suited her fine. Her last brush with romance had cured her of that particular dream for life. She was now a realist

— or perhaps would be for a year or so ... well, a few more months perhaps.

As she entered the apartment through her kitchen doorway, Jen placed the bowl of petals on her windowsill and wondered about them. What would it feel like if they were truly from a real Valentine, an admirer, or a new genuine lover of her own?

She realised that she really didn't care how long it took to find Mr Right, so long as she was able to steer clear of another Mr Wrong.

* * *

Reluctantly, after dinner had been eaten and she had mulled over the best course of action to take to solve the mystery of the petals, Jen picked up the phone. She did not want to leave the matter until the morning when there would only be a few free moments before the start of a new day in which to talk. Pressing the button, she watched the auto select bring up Sheila's number as it started to dial.

The phone at the other end rang and rang. Jen curled up on her two-seater sofa, dinner done, pots washed, and relaxed. With what was left of the glass of Merlot in her hand, she carefully balanced the phone against her ear.

This was what she thought of as her hour of sanity time before she did some preparation for the morning.

Looking around at her small living space, with its low glass coffee table, clean cream walls, neutral carpet and flat TV screen on the facing wall, she was lost in a moment of admiration. The uncluttered look made it feel so fresh. No discarded gym kits here.

With her head tilted back so that she could stare out at the evening sky, dark and starlit, she glanced at the bowl of petals adorning the low table.

'What a strange thing to do,' she murmured.

She could not imagine why anyone, even Sheila, would take the time to stand and slip petals carefully into a letter box like this. Perhaps she'd had them in a plastic bag and simply upended it into the mailbox. Whatever method was used, it would have required patience and care.

It just seemed bizarre, but perhaps, Jen thought, she had been giving the impression of feeling down after her dramatic split from Harris, when in fact, it had been due to tiredness because of finalising the details on the apartment and arranging the move.

The ringing tone stopped as the phone was answered. *Let it be Sheila*, she thought, just as another familiar voice spoke.

'Hi, Kevin speaking.'

Damn! she thought, and was tempted to put the phone down and hang up, but if she did the display would give her number as last call anyway.

'Hello?' he repeated.

'Hi, Kevin, sorry . . . I was distracted for a moment. Is Sheila there, please?' she asked, her voice unnaturally strained and artificially bouncy.

'Tell me who it is speaking, and I'll ask her,' he replied, his voice dripping sarcasm, since he clearly knew who it was.

'Very funny, Kevin. It's Jen, as well you know. Can you put her on for a moment?' Jen was still trying to be polite.

'Jen? Oh, yes, sorry, of course it is — 'that' Jen. How are you? It's been so long since we last met,' his voice taunted.

'Put her on the phone.'

Jen tried to stay calm. She had no time for him since the last Christmas party the four of them had attended.

Kevin knew Harris through the gym that Harris ran. It was Kevin and Sheila who had initially introduced them, no doubt with Sheila's encouragement; ever the matchmaker. The Christmas meal had turned out to be the last time the four of them had gone out together, as she and Harris had split up before the New Year.

'No 'please'? Don't they teach good

manners in school these days?' Kevin's tone was low, but she could hear movement in the background.

'I already said it . . . '

'She's just coming. Sorry to hear about you and Harris. Guess it's just another heart broken, eh, Jen? Here she is . . . Hope you like your new place. Catch up some time . . . ' His voice drifted off as Sheila took over the conversation.

'What's wrong, Jen?'

Jen could hear the distraction in Sheila's voice. She could also hear the family and Kevin talking and laughing in the background. It made her flat seem very quiet, unnaturally so, in some strange way. It was a feeling she did not care for. She downed the rest of her wine in one gulp and then swallowed.

'Have you really no idea, Sheila?' Jen asked, trying to relax after the brief and unwanted contact with Kevin.

Even without his physical presence near her, she found her grip tightened on the wine glass. Not wanting to break its twisted crystal stem and end her evening in the casualty department, she watched as her hand relaxed again, and then placed the glass carefully on the table.

'You speak in riddles, woman — what's up?' There was silence on the other end of the phone. 'Jen, you still there?' Sheila persisted.

'Petals?' Jen offered cryptically, as if they were playing a game of word association.

'Eh? Sorry, speak in sentences or give us a clue at least.' Sheila laughed.

'Do you know anything about some red rose petals that appeared in my mailbox late this afternoon?' Jen continued, wondering if this really was a prank by a stranger, even though it was too early for Valentine's Day.

'Nope, no idea at all. Just petals — on their own?' Sheila queried. 'As in no stems?'

'Yes, enough to fill up half of the space.'

'Who's a lucky lady then?' she asked, and laughed. 'How do you know that they came late in the afternoon?'

'They arrived later than the post, which doesn't arrive 'til then,' Jen replied.

'Right, never mind, I'll take your word for it, Poirot. Looks like someone loves you, eh?' She chuckled.

'Sheila, are you being straight with me? Are you sure you didn't do it, because it's a bit weird?' Jen paused at the notion, realising how weird it would be.

If Sheila had not put them there, then Jen would have no idea who had, unless they had been intended for one of the other flatmates. This triggered a new and more comforting possibility: they had been placed in the wrong mail box.

'Absolutely sure. I was with you, remember? Anyhow, where would I get money like that from on my pay?' Sheila asked.

Jen felt a little awkward. The difference between her teacher's pay

24

and the assistant's was broad, but then so was the level of training and responsibility.

There was a pause as Jen hesitated.

'Well, they're too early for 'V Day', anyway. Why don't you ask your neighbour if he saw someone fiddling with your post box? Surely he clocked them. Isn't he in the 'Noseyhood' watch?' Sheila asked and laughed at her own quip.

'Good idea. I will. He's usually around in the morning. I just thought I had best check with you first as you mentioned Valentine's Day and I guess I was hoping it was just a prank. See you tomorrow, then.'

Jen forced the bright tone back into her voice. It was as artificial to her own ears as it was apparently to her friend's

'You can't hide from love, Jen. They could be from Harris, you know.'

'Bye!' Jen did not want to know that.

'Hey — are you okay, Jen?'

'No worries. I'm fine. Bye. We'll talk tomorrow.'

Jen placed the phone quickly back on

the stand and stared at the petals, so lovely in her bowl, so delicate — and yet Jen was suddenly filled with a feeling of unease.

She remembered that her doors were unlocked and for some reason had a strong desire to secure her home. Pulling down the blinds, she decided she would ask Mr Marshall tomorrow if he had seen anyone come to her flat and pause a while by her mailbox. He would know who did it as he rarely missed anything.

Jen finished her glass of wine and looked at the petals — so mysterious — so odd.

'Wrong mailbox,' she declared to herself, and tried to feel as happy and content as she had been earlier in the day.

* * *

At 1a.m. the noise of a car outside the flat disturbed the peace as a door slammed.

Jen fell heavily, waking with a sudden jolt, or that was what it had felt like.

'No!' she screamed, panting erratically as she fought to get her bearings and to regain her composure.

The ceiling of her room came into focus as her hands gripped the duvet. She turned her head to the source of noise, realising she was in her new bedroom. Relieved, she breathed more evenly and stared at the bamboo window blind screening the starry dark sky from her vision. All of a sudden she had the strong desire to look out at the outside world.

The peace was spoilt when the silence beyond the window pane was broken by a solitary hiss, then a spit . . . then an ear-piercing shriek ensued — it was a cat fight!

Jen stared out across the park from her bedroom window. Sure enough the tabby from next door but one was defending its turf, giving full chase to some hapless stray from the park. Jen watched and shivered. Each noise seemed to tear at her nerves.

As she stared at the shadows for a while, she remembered what had really woken her up. It was not the cat's caterwauling; it was a word which had rebounded in her head, toying with her mind, tormenting her imagination until, in the privacy of sleep, the answer to the one word question — Why? — had been given to her.

Even Jen could not accept this. She'd had a dream — no, a nightmare where Harris was running after her, chasing her. It had started in a car park. She had locked up her Mini and was walking briskly to get away from him. He began to run. What could she do? She had run too, but to where? The surroundings were strange to her. Streets of tall buildings, closed shutters and locked doors faced her every which way she turned.

His voice had drifted to her on the air. 'Come back, Jen! Stay with me! I'm sorry! Please . . . '

He was begging her to stop, to go

back to live with him forever. She had increased her pace to almost running until her breath had burned in her chest.

Apologies began to flow from his mouth like a river of petals falling, cascading to the ground, leaving a trail.

A thought had crossed her mind as she darted down an alleyway between two tall walls running with cold water from a broken piece of guttering. That thought still haunted her that if people followed the trail of blood-red petals they would find her . . . or her body.

Jen shivered at the recall of the strange nightmare.

Outside her window pane the world was now still. Inside, in the privacy of her own flat, her mind was far from it. The recall tormented her soul: each petal that fell was a vibrant colour. As he closed the gap between them in his pursuit, her breath had hurt as it escaped from her lungs, filled with the fear and exhaustion of the chase.

Jen was standing, breathing deeply,

trying to force the sense of panic from her body as the inner movie played on, making her relive her own nightmare.

The petals had conjoined, the red had turned to liquid, and now flowed as a fountain of blood.

Renewed effort forced her onwards to another street and yet more closed doors. The viscous liquid threatened to splash the white nightgown she was wearing.

Jen held her sides. Wearing short pyjamas, she was as unlike the linen clad figure in her dream as could be, yet still it haunted her. It had felt so real, the chase . . . the blood . . . the fear.

The whole scene had turned into that of a gothic novel. Panting, stumbling, Jen had tripped, screaming as she landed on the cold earth. No buildings now, no sign of habitation and only one more life force present other than hers.

The fountain of blood had stopped, as time itself had, but red speckles of it had soiled her hem.

Jen gulped as she recalled screaming

like a wild animal — or the cat in chase. Harris had stood over her. He had fallen on top of her and she had woken as if she had landed from a great height onto her own mattress, moist from her perspiration, but with no sign of blood, nightgown or — thank goodness — Harris.

The chase, however, and her quickened heartbeat were all still so very real.

Standing by the window she inhaled deeply and evenly, trying to control her shaking body. The cause of the dream, she knew, was those bloody petals. Why would anyone, even with the best of intentions, give them to her? She did not crave anyone's attention, she wanted to be free — and she was, wasn't she? Jen told herself that she had no need of love, just wanted to be left alone, to discover who she really was again. If this was Harris's doing then she would . . .

No, there was nothing she could do! Talking to him would mean that his scheme had worked. No! Jen reasoned she was tired, fraught, and was letting her imagination run wild. He was out of her life now and would stay thay way.

She could not go back to bed as the sweat had been real. Instead, she turned on the shower and for the hundredth time or more — she had lost count of how many times she had scrubbed herself down — she washed away the memories of Harris and came out feeling clean and refreshed.

The soft Egyptian cotton towel rubbed against her skin gently, brushing it and seemingly cleansing her troubled mind. She remade her bed by replacing the sheets with crisp, freshly ironed ones and then flopped into it.

It was nearly 2a.m. — a few more hours' fitful sleep and Jen's new day would begin again. Only this time, Jen did not feel as happy as she had only one day earlier.

2

I arrived on time, woman. You are even later this morning! What happened to the ever punctual Jen? Yet again, my strike will not be now, but it will come, no fear. Here we go . . .

Tuesday 12th February 2013:

Target leaves apartment at 7.41a.m. Dressed practically and smart. Unlocks Mini Cooper. Throws heavy bag on back seat. Speaks to neighbour. Sits in driver's seat. Leaves. Manner: confident — not quite so relaxed — how things can so quickly change and believe me they will!

* * *

Jen slammed the car door shut after throwing her bag inside it. The nightmare had disturbed not only her sleep, but her peace of mind. She did not have a fanciful imagination or nature. Jen had prided herself on being a down to earth person. If she had a problem then she would deal with it head on, not whimper away in her sleep and wake up like a frightened rabbit — and an exhausted one at that.

Yet, she didn't really have a problem, did she? There was nothing to worry about, no problem for her to face. So why behave as if her old troubles were back?

She was completely over Harris, after all. He was gone from her life and she had her new home to enjoy. Just because someone placed a bunch of petals in the wrong damn mailbox, her mind had turned to mush. No! She would stop it now, before her life was controlled by irrational thoughts and fears. Obviously, she reasoned, the move had taken quite a lot out of her, and she still needed to build up her energy reserve.

She did not have any problems, not now that she was no longer at someone else's beck and call. So why had she let a stupid surprise gift, most likely not even meant for her, bring back yesterday's problems to her in such a graphic way? Besides, her nightmare was so wrong; she had not run away from Harris; Jen had openly walked out of his place and into one of her own.

She forced her shoulders back and smiled broadly at the world around her, controlling the urge to yawn. The past was where it belonged, behind her. Now to find out who it was that had really left her the collection of red petals.

'Mr Marshall . . . ' Jen shouted the name over the fence, which divided the house's garden from the land that the block of four apartments enjoyed as a garden space — devoid of all plants, though; just grass by the path and shingle on the short driveway. Well, it was February and Jen was no gardening expert but plants didn't seem to thrive in this cold month.

Seeing her neighbour nod in acknowledgment of her shout, she smiled at him. He had been sipping his tea as he admired his solitary patch of snowdrops in the centre of the lawn. As the year progressed they would be replaced by pansies.

Aware that time was ticking by, Jen decided to ask her question quickly, but without getting into a long explanation of what was happening in the neighbourhood. She was very aware of the fact that while he had plenty of time to chat, she did not.

'Morning, Jen — and please call me Bill; you know we're neighbours now. Neighbours, in the traditional sense of the word, should be friends also. The Good Book was right; we should love our neighbours as ourselves. The world would be a happier place, I feel, if we did. Although, it rather depends, I suppose, if we like ourselves in the first place.'

Jen nodded. She had wondered how anyone could love a stranger as yourself, but did not want to get pulled into a theological debate, so she just smiled at him politely as he stepped across to the fence. His smile was genuine enough, but there was something about his manner that seemed to command respect, perhaps more than a simple casual acquaintance deserved.

'Thanks . . . Bill. I wonder if you could tell me who put the . . . That is, if you saw anyone place anything in my mailbox yesterday afternoon.'

She watched his eyebrow rise and knew he instantly suspected foul play of some sort. Not wanting to start one of his rant-offs regarding the young teenagers who occasionally hung out in the park, she continued, 'Someone left me a small present, but forgot to leave a note or card to say who it was from. I just wondered if you noticed who it was.'

'I'm sorry to say, Jen, that I can't help you there. Normally, I might have been able to, but you see yesterday was the neighbourhood watch meeting at

Mrs Ashton's place down the road. You know how we're trying to enlist people into it. These days you can't be too careful. The poor swans were attacked over in the park last week. Hoodlums, I bet . . . ' he said angrily. 'They should bring back national service or put them in boot camp for a few months.'

'Sorry to cut in, Mr — Bill — but I just needed to ask the question before I left for work. I must go, or I'll be late for my class, and that would never do, would it?'

Jen smiled, as he nodded his understanding to her. Then she backed off quickly.

'CCTV! That's what's needed,' he shouted over to her as she walked to her car.

He waved to her as Jen slipped into the driver's seat. She had avoided being hooked into the neighbourhood watch scheme so soon, although it had been sweet of Mrs Ashton to send her a welcome card when she had moved in. Then the vigilant neighbour had wasted no time in giving her a flyer which gave the dates of the monthly meetings to be held all the way through until the summer.

Being impressed with the woman's use of Microsoft Publisher and her presentation, she had taken it to school. Sheila said that she admired the woman's forward thinking when Jen had shown it to her.

However, Jen had had to agree that it would take more than impressive leaflets to encourage more parents to join the parent/teacher's support group to raise funds for the school, but perhaps it would be a starting point if they had a few posters made along similar lines.

Jen drove more quickly than she usually did to make up the precious minutes lost to her normal routine and was not sure if her speed had been clocked by a mobile speed trap. She hoped not — only time would tell. She had only been a couple of miles over the limit, but that would make no difference to the fine if she had been caught.

*   *   *

She walked into the classroom feeling slightly lighter in mood than she had earlier when she left the apartment. Knowing she was going to be later than usual, she'd hoped to see that Sheila had already arrived and started laying out the games on the number table, but her heart sank when she realised that she was the first there.

Jen sighed as she saw Mr Finch, the headmaster, pass by her classroom door. It looked like today was going to be one of those days.

In a mad rush she quickly set to organising the games and sharpening the pencils before leaving out the children's books on the main table. Coffee would have to wait today.

A mere two minutes before the bell went, Sheila arrived, obviously flustered.

'So sorry, the car ahead had a blow out! I only stopped because I nearly rammed into her, but she was in such a panic that I waited until she'd called the AA before I left her. What a start to the day! I could murder a coffee . . . '

She gave Jen a hopeful sidelong glance.

'No chance.' Jen smiled at Sheila's crestfallen expression.

'Stupid woman!'

'Me?' Jen glanced sharply at her as she stared to sort out the rubbers.

'No, the woman who broke down! Anyway, are you OK this morning? Your phone call last night was a bit of a surprise. Petals, eh?'

She came over to Jen, despite there being only moments to the bell going.

'You sounded a bit strange last night. Even Kevin noticed it; he was concerned about you. Did you find out who left the petals? Strange it wasn't a complete bunch of flowers. I mean, were they plucked off or can you buy them like that?'

'I know, I wondered the same, but

then whole ones wouldn't fit in my mailbox.' She smiled, trying to make light of it. 'Listen, I'm fine. Someone will explain soon enough and then the 'mystery', if there is one, will be solved. Take a moment to sort yourself out while I see the children in, and then we'll chat at break.' Jen opened the door to let the first arrivals in.

Sheila, breathless and flustered, nodded and took her bag to the cloakroom.

Jen put her hand in her pocket and discovered her mobile. As soon as she could she discreetly pulled it out of her pocket, realising she had not switched it on since yesterday lunch time. She quickly did so, and then placed it high on the shelf above her table. It was not allowed in the classroom really because of the privacy rules and the need to protect the children from predatory photographers.

Strange world, Jen thought, but the reality was that technology represented danger as well as opportunity when in the wrong hands. She left it on, but in silent mode, instead of switching it off. Why? Even Jen was not sure, but she followed her instincts.

It was as she returned to the number table that Michelle's voice whispered to her.

'Miss Brightman, the star is shining by its own.'

The girl's eyes were wide and looking up at the reflected light making the foil star above shine. She was speaking low as if she did not want to alarm the other children.

'Thank you, Michelle. It's nothing to bother about.'

Jen lifted her mobile down from its place of hiding and glanced at its display.

'Miss Brightman,' Michelle shouted.

'Yes, what is it now?' Jen asked distractedly.

Michelle was now standing in the painting corner.

'Billie and Francis are fighting over the blue paint and I've told them they have to share. We all have to share things, don't we?' Michelle's voice intonated that superior tone, which her grandmother had obviously used when speaking to her, Jen thought.

Desperately wanting to look at her phone and see what the message was, Jen reluctantly slipped it back into her pocket out of sight and went over to Michelle.

The girl sounded like a recording of a grandmother's font of wisdom and old sayings. However, in this instance Michelle was right, but Jen wanted her to sound and behave more like a child, not a copy of an adult.

'Thank you, Michelle. Please help in the library corner. Emma might like to read a book with you.'

Michelle put her hands on her hips and shook her head at the two boys, before smiling at Jen because she had been given another task to do and happily walked off to see to it.

Jen waited for her to go across to the reading area and settle down next to the youngest child in the class, who had trouble pronouncing her phonics. She then turned her attention to the two boys.

'Now you two share, I know you can. If not, you might have to miss your outside play today to practise sharing.'

Jen saw them both register that she meant what she said; neither boy wanted to forgo their run around in the fresh air and they were suddenly able to remember how to take turns and share the equipment — at least for now, Jen thought.

Jen left them to it and slipped into the washroom, pulling out her phone. She had a message from an unknown number. Her finger hovered over the open button when Sheila shouted for her. Reluctantly the phone was slipped back into her pocket.

'Mr Finch, what can we do for you?' Jen smiled brightly at the headmaster of the school who was standing just inside the classroom. Normally, she was so professional, but today; today she just felt sleepy and distracted.

It was rare that the headmaster ventured around the classrooms so early in the day. One hand was behind his back, which gave his stance an unnatural look. His tall figure looked awkward in a room designed for such small people. Mr Finch glanced around at the children who were behaving quite well and all very busy with their given tasks.

'Good. All's well in here I take it?' he asked.

Jen smiled and, as he had, looked around at a harmonious classroom, which had various activities under way; from number play, painting, reading and Sheila on the mat arranging farm animals for the younger children. Relief and a modicum of pride swept through Jen. She was glad that he had not walked in a few minutes earlier, to see her standing there, mobile in her hand, whilst Michelle adjudicated over the blue paint debacle.

'May I have a word with you, Miss Brightman?' he said, pleasantly enough.

Sheila looked across, obviously curious. Jen did not know what the matter was, but she asked Sheila to take over as she stepped outside into the corridor with Mr Finch.

Jen was about to apologise for arriving later than usual, when he surprised her again, smiling broadly at her, and presented her with a black cardboard box tied with a beautiful red ribbon around it. On top of it was a solitary rosebud that had been fastened onto the ribbon with some wire from which hung a heart-shaped card, edged with gilt, upon which was a name written in copperplate writing: *Miss Jennifer Brightman xxx*

'I don't understand, Frank.' Jen looked at him bemused.

'I would like to claim they were from me, but Angela would be very upset if she thought I gave out such gifts to my female staff.' He chuckled.

Jen did not respond, as his wife did not strike her as a person with a broad sense of humour or understanding.

'They were delivered by hand, obviously meant for you. Jen, I do not wish to be a spoilsport, and I am delighted that you have an admirer. However, could I ask that he times such things a little better. If this is a Valentine's gift, then it's a couple of days early, and if it's your birthday then our records are wrong.'

'No, they're right, my birthday is in November. I have no idea who it's from. I have no idea who he is!'

Jen was reluctant to take the box from him. How could she explain that, far from being flattered by such an event, she was at the very least embarrassed to the point of becoming freaked out by this person's attention?

Whoever he was, he had intruded on her home space and now, it would appear, her work place also.

Forcing herself to smile, she politely accepted the box. It could only have half a dozen chocolates within it, but she was struck by the fact that, like the box, when she opened the lid and peeked inside, the chocolates seemed also to have been made by hand. Again, who would go to such trouble? Jen had no idea.

'I really don't understand who's doing this — or why,' she said quietly. She wanted Mr Finch to understand that this was totally unwanted attention.

'You're an attractive young woman. In my day that would have been sufficient reason.'

Jen looked up at him, surprised by his comment, even if it was as old-fashioned as it was unexpected, and saw his cheeks colour slightly.

Mr Finch turned abruptly to take a step away, his posture and manner suddenly changed.

'Jen, do try and make sure that at least one of you arrives on time. It was a close call this morning. Not good. Not good at all.' He shook his head slightly. 'You're normally here in good time. I rely on you.'

'Of course,' she said, cursing the fact

that he had been aware of her lapse.

Jen felt somehow undermined by these strange gifts, by the unforeseen circumstances and by time itself.

'Of course I will be. Like you say I normally am. The traffic was very bad this morning. There was a road closed by the bridge . . . caused a long tailback and . . . '

'Perhaps we could start our journeys a little earlier in order to compensate for such likelihoods,' he remarked and continued to walk away, but Jen — despite how peeved she was at being talked to like a child who needed to understand how to organise themselves — caught up with him.

'You couldn't tell me who delivered this, could you?' she asked, hoping that his answer would be a definite 'Yes', but as he shrugged, she knew this phantom giver of strange gifts was not going to be revealed so easily.

'I'm afraid not. It was left by the reception hatch when the new girl was in the office with me.' He looked at her thoughtfully and added, 'She's an agency girl who needed to be shown the ropes. That's another thing . . . to be honest with you, Jennifer, I don't like the fact that a stranger entered and left the school unnoticed, leaving a package behind. This is innocent enough, but people like to think they've left their children in a secure environment. Imagine if that parcel had held menace!'

Jen nodded. She knew how seriously Mr Finch took security matters, but his body language seemed to relax after his sterner moment.

'You'll just have to wait until Thursday, I fear, to see who your admirer is,' he said at length and then he glanced back to her classroom and she took the hint.

'Yes, I suppose so. I can't wait,' she said with no enthusiasm or conviction. All she wanted to do was to tell him — whoever he was — to leave her alone.

Jen returned to the classroom as

curious eyes watched her. She placed the box on her table and stared at it for a minute before snapping back to what she had been going to do before the interruption.

* * *

Jen's break had been filled with catching up with jobs and had gone so quickly that neither she nor Sheila had had a child-free moment to talk to each other.

It was lunchtime before she managed to get a break long enough for her to check the inbox on her phone. When she did, she read the brief message and froze.

Roses are red . . .

'What?' she exclaimed, and then realised when she checked the detail that it had been sent to her the previous evening, but she had only switched her phone on when she arrived at school today, so she hadn't received the text when she had been intended to.

'The petals!' she repeated 'The damn petals!'

The phone slipped from her fingers onto the table next to her latest gift.

As Sheila arrived and looked at both the message and the chocolates, she grinned broadly.

'You are a lucky girl!' she said. 'Someone has gone to a lot of trouble for you. Can I take a look?'

Jen nodded, although she was quite happy to tell her to take them. She did not want anyone messing with her day. Jen was just escaping from a bad relationship and she did not want to be pestered in this manner by anyone, not now. Anonymity was what she craved.

Sheila started to pull the ribbon loose.

'Don't you find this all a bit creepy?' Jen asked.

'What? Having petals scattered at your feet and then chocolates being delivered by hand — not to mention that this guy has a poetic streak and a crazy sense of timing.' Sheila looked skyward. 'If Kevin had done this sort of thing for me, I would have melted into his arms.'

'You did anyway,' Jen said in a matter of fact manner.

Sheila laughed. 'Well he'll have to wait until I get those earrings . . . ' She winked.

'Too much information!'

Jen swallowed; she did not smile though. If Kevin could be bothered to do this for Sheila then fair enough. It would be a game they would both enjoy. But she did not have a 'Kevin' in her life — thank goodness.

Jen could not rid herself of the feeling of dread that threatened to engulf her. It was her privacy that was gradually being eroded.

Now 'he' had her mobile phone number too. Who, other than Harris, had this information? Then she remembered she'd switched sim cards after breaking up with him because of his relentless texts, so even he didn't have her new number.

Sheila lifted the rose, ribbon and tag off the box so that they could open it properly and take a proper look inside. Six handmade dark chocolate sweets, shaped as if there were a cherry inside them, had been arranged on black tissue paper in their own small gold mini cake case. Atop each one was a small candied flower.

'Oh, how cute are they?' Sheila exclaimed. 'I'll pop the kettle on while you sample a choccy!' She paused and then added, 'Save one for me!'

Jen did not want to touch them, but simply stared at them. She was not flattered and she wanted none of this. In fact she dreaded to think whose hands had actually shaped them.

Her phone beeped again.

Another message — from the same number. As she stared at the small blue flowers on top of each sweet, she somehow knew what it was going to say, but as she pressed the button to reveal the words, it was as if her pulse slowed and time had also slowed down to join it.

Violets are blue . . .

Snapping back into reality, Jen quickly picked up her mobile and rang the number.

She was through with waiting and letting this guy play with her like a puppet, pulling her strings; whoever it was, he was going to be told straight that this was not the way to get her attention in a positive way. If he was genuinely interested then he should come forward or at least wait until Valentine's Day arrived. It just felt so wrong, like being pestered.

'Sorry, the number that you are dialling is currently unavailable . . . '

Jen switched off her phone and placed it back on the shelf.

'Damn!' she muttered angrily.

Never mind, she told herself. She had the number and would keep trying it until she got through. He was not as clever as he thought he was.

'Miss Brightman!'

The shout from outside in the play area was ominous.

'Yes?' she answered, as she grabbed her jacket and made her way outside.

'Ben's fallen off the climbing frame and scuffed his knee!'

Jen sighed and comforted the lad, who seemed more shaken than actually hurt. Fortunately, it was no more than a bloodied graze, but it needed seeing to.

Ten minutes later she returned to her chair, just as Sheila came back. Jen and Sheila approached together. Two mugs of coffee were put down next to the table by the box of chocolates.

'Well, what are you waiting for?' Sheila asked anxiously; obviously in anticipation of savouring one.

Emma had wandered back into the classroom with Michelle following behind her.

They saw the chocolate box and came over, looking at them with curiosity.

'Pwetty,' Emma said.

'Pretty,' Michelle corrected her.

'Aren't you going to have one?' Sheila asked.

'No. I'm off chocolate at the moment.'

Jen saw Sheila's expression change to one of disappointment, so she picked up the box and offered her one. 'Feel free,' she said.

Sheila picked one up. It was as if she felt guilty taking one of these 'precious' gifts from her friend. She lifted the chocolate up carefully and winked at the children who watched in anticipation, no doubt in hope that they too may be rewarded with one.

Suddenly Emma's scream made Jen drop the box and Sheila stop mid air with the chocolate between her fingers.

'Worm!' Emma shouted, and pointed at the bottom of the chocolate in between Sheila's fingers.

'What!' Sheila exclaimed in shock.

Jen stared as something fell from the underside of the sweet onto the table. She stared at it and at another obnoxious wriggly creature in the bottom of the golden cake case that the sweet had been lifted from, and swallowed.

'That's a grub . . . a maggot,' Michelle explained to her friend. 'Worms are longer.'

Sheila threw the sweet into the bin and nearly fell backwards off the stool as she gulped.

'That's gross! Who put that in there?'

Sheila looked around as the rest of children filed back in.

'Michelle, did you see anyone interfere with this box while I saw to Ben?' Jen asked.

'No, I didn't.' She looked up at Sheila's accusing stare. 'I didn't put it there, honest . . . I know it's a maggot because my uncle goes fishing with them.'

She looked stricken as if she were being suspected.

Jen threw the box and the maggots into a plastic bag and knotted the top. Fortunately, she always had a supply on hand for little 'accidents' within the classroom. It paid to be prepared when working with young children.

'Sheila, calm Emma down, please. Give her one of the rewards from the treats bag and let's get on with the day.'

Jen dismissed any further attempts at conversation on the subject for now. She had a room full of impressionable youngsters to care for and now was not the time for histrionics.

* * *

Jen sat down, feeling exhausted as the last student left for the day.

'One of them will have done it as a prank.' Sheila looked at Jen. 'They're kids and some of the lads are so naughty — actually a few of the girls would be capable of it. Michelle . . . '

'They're so young. Young kids don't like maggots, Sheila, and even if they do, they wouldn't interfere with things like this. They'd just drop them in the box at worst not place them carefully underneath the chocolate. What if they didn't do this? Do you even get maggots like that in a garden?'

Jen looked at her friend, who was staring at her as if she was worried about Jen's mental state.

Jen got one of the painting palette knives and discreetly opened the carrier bag. She had to know if the maggots had come from inside the sweets. She squished one of the chocolates. Nothing but fondant oozed out, the flower fell off and there was no hidden fruit inside — and nothing 'maggoty' secreted within it.

'They won't be from the garden, but fish food is more than possible. Mrs Skelton uses them as a supplement for the fishes in the entrance hall and corridors. They're kept in the storeroom next to our washroom.'

Sheila placed a conciliatory hand on Jen's shoulder.

'It may have spoilt what was meant as a lovely gesture, but really there's no great mystery here. We'll cancel playtime tomorrow and see if one of them owns up. That Michelle is always on hand when anything funny happens. She'd be my first suspect — and she's fed the fish before too. She always wants to do everything.'

'No. Michelle is awkward sometimes, but not nasty. Could they have been delivered with the maggots already in there?' Jen asked pensively.

'No way! You've watched too many whodunnits.' Sheila laughed at Jen's theory.

'But how do you explain the texts?' Jen had not meant to sound as alarmed as she did. 'I should tell Mr Finch. This is all too weird.'

'I wouldn't,' Sheila said. 'How would you explain you had a mobile phone on in the classroom? You know how keen he is that we obey the rules. Also, how do you explain to him that the maggots were left in such an accessible place without getting your colleague, poor Louise Skelton into trouble? She loves looking after the fish and takes pride that she knows what's best for them.'

Sheila sighed and went on, 'Jen, I'm sorry. I shouldn't have left the chocolates open like that. Now they're all spoilt.'

She picked up the knotted carrier bag.

'I'll get rid of this. You go back to your lovely flat. Take a long soak in that new bath of yours and relax. You're just overtired,' she advised. 'Just you wait and see — in a couple of days' time this will all be shown to be no more than a well meaning gesture by someone who obviously thinks a lot about you. Go home and relax. Have some wine and chill out.'

Jen smiled and nodded but was far from convinced.

Maggots! Louise must be the one teacher who did not cringe at the things. A wave of nausea swept through Jen as she visualised Sheila raising the chocolate towards her mouth . . .

Thank goodness Emma was watching. Normally, it was the eagle-eyed Michelle who saw things first. Her eyes must have been fixed on those choco-lates left in the box.

Sheila left. Jen was collecting up her last papers and putting them into her bag, when she noticed the discarded heart-shaped card. As she'd gathered her papers, the card had fallen on the floor.

Looking at the the words again, it seemed to Jen so carefully written. She was just about to toss it into the bin, but changed her mind and picked it up.

Holding it in her fingers by its edge and reaching up to the shelf, she slipped it there out of sight.

If it was all part of an innocent prank then she might be able to look upon it again someday, but only if it was part of a prank, and something told her it was more sinister than that.

As Jen left her room, switching off the lights, she walked down the lonely corridor trying to shake off the doubt that that one word triggered in her mind — if.

Arriving back at her apartment Jen approached her mailbox with strong feelings of suspicion. She slowly turned the key and let the flap fall open. There were no petals, nothing unusual, just a bill — never had Jen been so relieved to receive one of those before.

She secured the box and collected her bag from the car before turning to walk down the side of the building to her door. Only two steps into the darkened alleyway she saw a figure move ahead of her.

Instantly, she took two quick steps backwards, ready to flee to her neighbour's house.

'Sorry, miss,' the voice said. 'I didn't mean to frighten you. The bulb has gone out in the security light, so I decided to replace it.'

The voice was male, sounded confident and polite, but was not one she was familiar with though. The detached words were quite well spoken, lacking a trace of the local accent, while they continued to explain his presence.

Jen watched as she saw a figure come forward towards her, taking shape as it stepped into the glow from the street light.

He was smartly dressed in a casual manner; tall, wearing a black full zip leather jacket that somehow accentuated the depth of his brown eyes and darkness of his short hair.

Jen glanced down, relieved, and took a deep breath. She noticed his jeans, nicely cut, and the tough looking black leather work boots.

'Of course . . . good,' Jen answered. Looking up again she met his eyes. Dark, thoughtful and direct, she thought. Yet she felt as though, if he said 'Boo!', she would flee in a trice.

'Is there something wrong, miss?' he asked. 'I live upstairs, in number two.'

He looked a little concerned and confused by her reaction to his presence.

'No . . . nothing at all. Sorry, I didn't

realise you were my neighbour that's all. I thought . . . Sorry, it's been a very busy day.' She relaxed and smiled at him. 'I'm Jen, from number one. We haven't met before.'

Jen held out a hand, feeling as though she had gone into ultra-polite mode. They were standing in the half light on her drive, for goodness sake, not in a formal meeting room. What would he think of his new, slightly neurotic neighbour?

Nevertheless, he shook her hand formally and she saw him grin. 'Pleased to meet you, Jen.'

Jen pulled her hand away and gestured that she wanted to go inside, taking a small step backward. 'You too.'

The man stood aside as Jen walked past him to open her own door.

'Perhaps we could have coffee some time?' he asked, as she entered her sanctuary.

'Yes.' She looked back fleetingly. 'Perhaps some time. Bye.'

Jen shut the door quickly behind her,

before he could suggest a time or place — or offer some corny pick-up line, like 'Your place or mine?'

He lived too close to her for her to even consider becoming involved, even in a neighbourly, friendly way.

Jen wanted space. She knew what it was to have someone hound your every moment that you were free, demanding that they knew where you were, when you'd be back, or sulking if you were out when they were in.

Then there was the endless suspicion, the questions, the doubting of her and the need of reassurance — and for what? To suffer betrayal at their hands? No, Jen had little intention of letting anyone so close to her get to know her, especially from a polite handshake.

She locked the door from the inside, dropping the key into her handbag, and left him to finish his job in the narrow alleyway between the house and the apartments.

Within minutes a glow from the

security light shone through the half-paned door, showing Jen that he had fixed the light.

A thought struck her. Perhaps he had seen who had put the petals in the mailbox the day before. It was just a chance, but she also realised he had not given her his name, either.

She fumbled in her bag for her door key. Why had she not left them hanging in the door? She opened it wide and poked her head outside, but he had gone.

She thought about knocking on the door of number two, but as she glanced up she could see the lights were all off.

For a moment even this seemed strange to her. It was then she heard the motor bike being driven off and saw the back of his leather jacket visible as he sped away down the road.

'Oh well.' Jen shrugged telling herself that tomorrow was another day.

She returned to her flat, safe and secure, wondering if she should be less uptight and offer him a cup of coffee if their paths crossed at the weekend. Besides, she might owe him something for fixing the light; it was part of the shared area of the apartment block.

3

So, Ms Brightman, how are we doing this morning? Taps the dashboard in anticipation. Here we go . . .

Wednesday 13th February 2013:

Target leaves apartment at 7.20a.m. precisely. Manner: pensive — excellent! Last observation — This is working. Now fate can take over.

★   ★   ★

Jen woke up slightly earlier than usual, but decided not to lie in, not after being caught out yesterday by Frank Finch. He had his little foibles and two of them were punctuality and security.

Not feeling as fresh and ready for the day as she would have liked, at least she had slept without being chased by a petal spewing ex-fiancé. The thought of her imagination playing such warped tricks on her mind, when it was supposed to be at rest, actually brought half a smile to her face.

What a wuss she had turned into! Perhaps she should just accept that it would take a little while for her to put the last year's experience behind her and ease up a bit. It could be that she needed a little flirtation in her life again, so long as it was at a distance and not on her doorstep — her new lovely doorstep.

How she wished that it was the weekend and not the half-way point of the week. As she walked across her living-room to open the window blind she saw the bowl of petals still on her coffee table.

'Sorry, you may be beautiful, but I don't want you in my apartment or my life.'

She laughed at the thought that she was now talking to an inanimate object as she picked them up, tipped them into her kitchen waste bin and washed and stacked the bowl on the drainer. She had never been one to give in to superstition, but since they had arrived, her life seemed to have been overcast by a shadow and she wanted to bask in the sunshine again.

That done, she dressed, ready for the day ahead. The thought that yet more disruption to her routine should occur made her shiver involuntarily. It was no good, she must be hormonal or something. Things were starting to freak her out so quickly — but why? Perhaps the dream had been right in one way. She suspected that Harris would seek her out again and her own inner worry was causing her unrest.

Looking out of her window as she collected a file from the table she felt her spirits lift. The sun was indeed shining. She wanted to feel its warming welcome, so hurried up.

Stepping outside she remembered it was February and made a 'note to self' to order her holiday brochure. Hong

Kong, she thought to herself; somewhere exotic, developed and different — so different to anywhere she had ever been. This time, though, she would be going on her own.

The crisp sunshine surprised her with the chill it held. She glanced around. No sign of anyone there, yet she had an uneasy feeling that she was being watched. Jen shrugged it off as she saw Mr Marshall wave to her from the other side of his garden. Of course she was being watched! When did he ever stop watching what was happening? The strange thing was, though, that Mr M looking on like some all-knowing father figure usually gave her a good friendly feeling.

She sat behind the wheel of her car and wondered if she should ask him about her neighbour at number two, then checked her apparently growing tendency to flights of paranoid fancy, and drove off.

★ ★ ★

Her day started remarkably uneventfully after the previous two, which pleased Jen immensely. Sheila seemed content to stop talking about 'V Day' and the maggot experience was only mentioned at lunch time — ironically. The mere mention of them was enough to put Jen off her chicken wrap.

'You know we can't really have an inquisition over what happened yesterday,' Sheila said.

'I've had a word with Louise about using them — you know, the live maggots as fish food. Mr Finch wouldn't approve. Besides, we have no idea if the children actually touched them. Anyway they shouldn't be so accessible.' Jen rationalised. 'I'll speak to Michelle when she's waiting for her grandmother to arrive and see if she knows anything more, but I really don't think it was her.'

'You'd believe her?' Sheila asked, with a raised eyebrow.

Jen was surprised by her response. 'Yes, why ever not?'

'I don't. She lurks in corners and watches and, you know, eavesdrops on the other kids. It's not natural behaviour, is it?'

Jen thought for a moment.

'She mimics her grandmother and wants to act like an adult, that's all. She copies what we do in a way, or what she has seen her grandmother do, I suspect. That's why I don't think she would do something so childish and wicked as play a prank like that. Besides, I still think they were put in there to start with.'

Jen saw Sheila sit back in horror at the idea. Then she shook her head and stood up. Next she patted Jen's back as she took a step away.

'You need to lighten up,' she said. 'Seriously, you're in need of some 'love' therapy, especially since 'V Day' is nearly here. My earrings will soon be in my hand — or ears — and you'll discover what someone special really thinks of you.'

Sheila wandered off to take her turn

at playground duty. Jen watched her go, feeling as though she had just been treated like one of the children.

A noise from the book corner took her attention as something dropped to the floor, and then she caught sight of a slight movement. Jen stood up and walked over.

Her intuition was not wrong. Looking over the partition she saw the curled up figure of Michelle clinging to a story book, eyes wide and slightly moist.

'Michelle! Why aren't you outside with the other children?' Jen deliberately kept her voice low and soft.

The girl looked close to tears.

'You were listening, weren't you?' Jen added, knowing full well that while the girl had been caught out by her teacher, the teachers had been, in a way, caught out by her.

Thank goodness it had not been Sheila who discovered her.

The girl nodded.

'Come here,' Jen said carefully and took the girl by the hand and sat down on the special chair she used to read to the children individually.

'Tell me honestly, did you place the maggots in the chocolate box?' she asked.

'No, Miss Brightman. I wouldn't, but *you* know that.'

Michelle glanced in the direction of the playground; not saying what she would like to about Sheila, but Jen could guess that the girl had been hurt by Sheila's comments.

'Do you know if anyone else did? The truth, Michelle, I just need to know,' Jen asked, but the girl kept her mouth closed and shook her head.

'Why are you in here, instead of playing with the other children? You know you're supposed to go out too.'

Michelle nodded.

'They're so . . . childish . . . ' she sniffed.

Jen could not help but smile at her.

'They're supposed to be. They're children — like you. They play games and have fun. Sometimes they may bicker, but it's all part of being children. Even adults can behave like children occasionally — it's allowed. Now go and get your coat and run and play with the others. Have some fun and stop trying to be like us — you'll grow up soon enough.'

Michelle smiled and Jen realised that it was what the girl wanted to hear. Why was she being told to grow up before her time? Or at least that was what it seemed like to Jen.

'Thank you, Miss Brightman,' she said, and sniffed again.

'Michelle, which park did you mean when you asked if I went to play in one?'

The girl smiled broadly as she buttoned up her coat. 'Ours. It has ducks.' She quickly pulled on her hat and then ran out of the door.

Jen stared after her as she ran off to the playground.

Did she mean 'ours' as in hers and her grandmother's, or theirs and Jen's. She wondered if it was the same park and thought that she should look up the girl's address and see if it had changed. Or did everyone know where she now lived?

★　★　★

Jen was relieved that no more deliveries had arrived at the school nor in her mailbox.

She felt fairly relaxed again and had enjoyed preparing her own food. She placed her pasta on her plate next to the arranged salad, and then added the chicken in pesto sauce on top. She had really fancied fish and chips, but this was healthier and she didn't want to start comfort eating. Besides, she was in her own apartment and eating off her new white porcelain plates — not Ikea's, but bought from the department store's china department.

Sitting at her kitchen table she saw a shadow go past her door. Instantly, Jen was standing up. Her door was locked, a precaution she did every time she entered. She wondered why the security light had not flashed on, lighting up the back of the grounds and the alleyway.

She stood there waiting, then she heard the door of the next flat open and shut and she sighed. What was she like? Jumping at shadows!

Jen poured herself her daily allowed glass of wine and picked up her fork, dropping it the moment her doorbell rang. She stood up again, thinking that at this rate she would need more than wine to calm her nerves.

Reluctantly she left her dinner and opened her door. Mr Marshall stood there, holding a wine bottle in his hand.

'Mr Marshall, what a surprise.'

Jen wondered what he was doing with it. He was too short to have cast the earlier shadow. She casually glanced up and saw that the light was on in flat number two. She smiled; shadow mystery solved.

'Hello, Jen. Remember you're supposed to be calling me Bill.' He smiled, obviously thinking her smile had been for him.

'Yes, sorry, Bill. Is something the matter?' she asked.

'Not really. It's just that this was left outside the side gate. I thought I had better remove it. Asking for trouble, I'm afraid, leaving it there. Thought you must have put it down when you were bringing your things in from the car. It's just that if those hoodlums see it they could just as easy drink the contents and smash the glass all over the drive.

Jen felt the same unease sweep through her as she had when the chocolates arrived. 'No, it's not mine. I think it's possibly my neighbour's at number two. He must have put it down before he went in and forgotten to pick it up.'

'Oh no, it's definitely for you . . . Look.'

He held up a heart shaped gilt edged card on which was written a simple message in copper plate: *Miss Jennifer Brightman xxx*

'Thank you, Bill. Why don't you take it as a thank you from me for being so vigilant?' Jen saw his eyes widen.

'I couldn't possibly do that, but I appreciate the offer. I won't keep you. Here you are, you enjoy it.'

He handed her the bottle and smiled before walking off.

Quickly Jen locked the door. This had to stop! Thank goodness Valentine's Day would be the next day. The mystery would be solved. If it was Harris she might have to look at some sort of legal way of keeping him away from her — not knowing if there was one for someone just being a nuisance. If it was a new person, then he was not for her. His 'gifts' freaked her out.

Maggots — were they in the box first or not? Now this had arrived, a bottle of wine.

A sudden thought occurred; this was not from Harris — he knew she drank red wine and this was rosé. It was cheap plonk.

Jen put her hand in her bag and

switched on her phone. It was still off from being in the classroom. She watched and waited as it lit up.

The label on the bottle was pretty and read, 'Rosé — a sweet dessert wine — a rich wine full of grapey, floral flavours.'

'How apt!' she said as a text message beeped its arrival. The message was again predictable.

. . . sugar is sweet . . .

She quickly called the sender, but unfortunately the message there was also predictable too: 'Sorry, the number you are dialling is currently unavailable . . . '

4

The doorbell rang just as Jen was putting her cereal into her bowl. It was Valentine's Day — the dreaded 'V Day' — yet, as she approached the door, she was aware of a lightening inside her; the knowledge that all would be revealed to her at last swept a feeling of relief through her whole body.

The last few days had been tense and had caused her more than enough pain. She was supposed to be celebrating freedom, being unattached and enjoying the ensuing peace that should follow — not living in fear of shadows of the unknown.

Jen opened the door just as a police car seemed to be pulling away across the road and she rationalised that 'hoodlum' activity must indeed be on the rise. Instantly, she wondered if last night's shadow had been that of her neighbour after all.

A delivery lady was standing in front of her holding out a large bunch of flowers. Her plain white van was adorned by an illustration of a bouquet with a simple livery on its side. *Anastasia's Blooms* adorned the ribbon that swept around the simplistic design. Jen looked at the woman's tired face as she held out a bouquet of ten red stem roses and smiled.

'Special delivery for you,' she said, as she glanced at the card which came with them. 'Miss Brightman.'

'Thank you. Can you tell me who they're from?' she asked hopefully, as the woman began to walk away.

'There's a card inside.' The woman winked at her. 'He's quite a catch though, if you don't mind my saying so. Nice biceps.' She winked at Jen and wasted no time in driving off.

Harris, Jen thought.

'They're absolutely beautiful,' said Mr Marshall's voice in admiration. He knew his flowers and Jen had to agree with him, these were lovely and must have cost a small fortune.

Jen looked across the fence and saw him standing there in his Fair Isle jumper and tweed jacket, mug in hand as he surveyed his garden.

'Wish I was twenty years younger,' he said and laughed in a good-natured way. 'Alright, maybe forty, if I'm honest, eh?'

'Bill, I'm flattered,' she said and he laughed. 'Thirty at a push,' she added and was rewarded with another chuckle.

Jen was lost in the moment as she looked at the beauty of the buds. So tight, so perfect and so utterly beautiful.

Catching a glimpse of the time on her watch, she raised the flowers up, looked at Mr Marshall and then quickly took them inside to her kitchen.

A small card fell out as she placed them carefully on top of the table. There was no point in wasting good flowers, she thought, so she filled up the only vase she possessed which was big enough to take them with cold water and speedily dropped them into it. With the wrapping discarded, she thought, she would play at arranging them on her return home.

The card in a tiny envelope was the last thing she picked up. Well the time of revelation was here — it was now — the mystery would be revealed and she would find out the truth of it.

It had to be Harris, the biceps reference was so him. She placed her phone on the table next to the vase, switched it on and rang the number of the previous messages. If they were going to send her another message now, then she would catch them out. She pressed the 'call' button.

'The number you are dialling is currently unavailable . . . '

'Damn!'

Jen ripped open the card, annoyed that her little plan had not worked. She had tried the number twenty times or more in the last twenty-four hours and always it was unavailable.

As she pulled out the card she was

disappointed that she did not see another heart-shaped message in the same script as the other two. To her surprise it bore no resemblance to the previous days' 'gifts'. She had hoped it would since that would have made things so much simpler. Better the enemy you know, after all.

The card had a heart on its front and, in familiar ungainly writing, the message was simple, and heartfelt no doubt, but it did not touch Jen in that way. Instead, she was strangely detached from it and the plea it held.

For my darling Jen. Come home. Please! H x

Jen swallowed. Despite her best efforts she did fill up with emotions, but not of love and loss, more of fear and dread. She took a minute to compose herself, knowing she had to get to work soon.

She sent a quick text to Sheila's phone: *Running a few minutes late — cover for me. Be there soon. Dentist. OK?*

Even though Jen expected the phone to beep with Sheila's reply, as it did when there was a message coming in, it still made her jump. She stroked one of the rose's soft petals as she opened the message.

So, are you . . . ?

Jen stared at it for a second. What? She hit the call button.

'The number you are dialling is currently unavailable . . . '

'Damn! Damn! They must switch the thing off the very second it's sent!'

She scrunched up the envelope that the card had come in and tossed it into the waste-bin. Was it Harris? If so, why? He had sent her the flowers and said what he wanted to openly without any mystery at all.

Jen was annoyed that he had contacted her at all at her new address, despite her demands that he left her alone, but why the text? Why would he send such a thing? It was too over-worked for him — he was more blunt.

Who the hell was messing with her? She needed to know.

The phone beeped again. Jen jumped as she picked it up, ready to hit 'call'. Opening the message she realised that this one was from her friend, not a foe.

No worries. Finch is at a council meeting this morning and won't be back till nearly lunch, so his new girl has informed me. You OK?

The message was from Sheila. There was no point in sharing the news of her latest arrival just yet. Sheila would no doubt try to use it as a reason for Jen to patch things up with Harris, as he and Kevin were gym mates and it had been such a cosy arrangement for them to have partners who worked together too.

How could Jen explain to Sheila, without offending her long-term work colleague and friend, that to her it was claustrophobic? That was the word she would have chosen to describe the entire relationship, in fact. Not only that, but then there was Kevin to deal with. His behaviour had really shocked her and she cringed as she remembered his attempt at a drunken fumble with her.

Jen looked at the phone.

'Surely he wouldn't play a stunt like this?'

She looked at the message again.

'Am I sweet? Good question!' she said to herself, and then saw the time on her cooker's digital display — 7.52a.m. 'Damn!'

Jen left the card where it fell, picked up her phone, bag, jacket and keys and headed for the door.

With moist eyes, feeling unbelievably vulnerable, she drove away. The flowers were beautiful, there was no denying that and they would have been expensive, but she could not be bought back. There had been good times, initially, with Harris, but not for that long before his possessive side had come through.

If he could have been like he was when they had first started dating, he would have still had her there at his side, in his home, sharing his bed. How had she stayed with him for so long? She had no idea. She had felt trapped. Little by little he had eaten away at her confidence. However, she had fought back, because she had more about her than to be a bully's puppet.

★ ★ ★

Jen was relieved to see that Mr Finch's car space was empty. Let's see what today brings, she thought, as she made her way into a classroom which was as busy and vibrant as always.

Sheila had a group of children painting heart shapes on a long table covered with newspapers. Initially, it had seemed such a good idea when Jen had planned it. Now it was like salt applied to a very raw and open wound.

'Hi,' Jen said, as she discreetly dropped her things in her cupboard, and then walked over to where Sheila was.

'Haven't we been busy?' Jen said.

Her eyes were dry now and she was doing her utmost best to blank out everything that had happened and focus only on what she needed to do to get through the day.

'Sure have, so what held you up?' Sheila asked, as they walked away to check on the progress in the farm. This was a floor activity which had its own carpet laid out with the fields, pens and animals for a very pretty farm layout of yesteryear. No battery hens or mass milking sheds here.

'Perhaps we should have the figures from the Lego play kit protesting on the edge of the mat against the terrible pricing of milk?' Jen said quietly.

'Cynic!' Sheila said. 'Well, what kept you this morning — more gifts?' Sheila raised quizzical brows. 'You're lucky that Finch was out or you would have been on his naughty step!' She laughed, but Jen did not.

Jen looked at her. 'You're not wearing your earrings? Did he not surprise you then?'

She desperately wanted to change the focus of the conversation. To stay on safe ground away from her problems.

'There was only time for the cards and chocolates this morning. However, there's time and opportunity to come as we're having a meal out this evening. He's picking me up here after school. He needs the car for a few days, so I have a chauffeur for a while.'

Sheila's face was very animated.

'I can't wait. I'm going to feel like a proper lady by the end of today! Mum's helping out with the kids, so we can stay out late, come home when we want and have the place to ourselves. Might be a good idea if we actually came back earlier and made use of the opportunity . . . '

She winked but when Jen didn't respond, she added, 'So why were you late?'

'I had a delivery of red roses from Harris.' Jen didn't look at Sheila straight away. 'I had to put them in water.' She thought she might as well come clean as put up with a whole day of speculation and questions.

'Aw, he really misses you. Kev says that he — '

'Ben, how is your knee today?'

Jen cut across Sheila's comment, regretting she had ever had the stupidity to tell her the truth. Why hadn't she just made up a lie? People do all the time; why should she be different?

'My knee's still sore, Miss Brightman,' Ben replied sadly.

'Maybe you need a bravery sticker! Come over to the treats bag. I think you deserve one.'

★   ★   ★

Jen took over the rest of the activities, leaving Sheila to manage the production of the Valentine Cards, which had been made mainly for their mums.

Jen was now trying to come to terms with the fact that she would have to face another demon — Kevin was arriving to pick up Sheila at the end of the day. She wondered if the week could get any more challenging. She had been late in and so could not find a reason or way to justify ducking out early and avoiding him and besides, she needed to be there when the children left.

As soon as playtime arrived, she avoided Sheila again by taking a comfort break.

Jen had kept her phone in her pocket and she took it into the washroom with her, trying one more time, but when she pressed 'call' she still got the same message, 'The number you are dialling is currently unavailable . . . '

Jen held her head back, breathed deeply and stared at the sky through the narrow window, which was placed high in the wall. A white cloud floated by in a blue sky, shortly followed by a darker grey and more menacing one. That was how her week had been. It had started so bright, she was so full of optimism and desires to forge this new life for herself, but her old one was not letting go.

Then there were these silly gifts. If they were not from Harris, then who were they from?

Jen read the messages again. One after the other ... *Roses are red ... Violets are blue ... Sugar is sweet ... So, are you?*

Whoever had written these had changed the last message from a statement into a question. Jen had never claimed to be 'sweet'. She wondered if she should report it to the police, but was not sure what she would say if she did — after all, there was no threat, even if she did sense that there was menace there.

When Sheila walked in, she was still staring at the phone.

'Break's over, Jen. Louise is covering. What the hell is going on with you?' She took the phone from her friend.

Reading the messages for herself, she looked up at Jen. 'So, what is the big deal? Harris loves you and it could be his desperate plea to get you back.'

'Perhaps. The flowers were from him, but these messages — I don't think so. They're not his style.' Jen held her hand out for the phone.

'How can you be sure?' Sheila asked, as she flicked through them again.

'I never gave him my new number, for one. Take care, Sheila, the touch pad is sensitive on that phone. I still prefer buttons.'

'He could have got it, though. I mean, I have it. Kev could have looked it up for his mate. He knows what this is doing to him and he's been worried about him. He's not training like he used to, you know.'

She sighed heavily before she went on, 'Look, he's suffering and quite frankly, Jen, you really are becoming a bit of a mess, aren't you? Why don't you see him? Phone the number and if he has sent these messages to you then you can put it right.'

'I can never get through,' Jen admitted. 'Besides, it's not his number.'

'You changed yours, Jen. He could have changed his.'

'Sheila, you know I value our friendship, but you don't understand what he's really like. I can't go back to being controlled, manipulated and . . . well, never mind.'

Jen paused and sighed heavily. 'Believe me when I tell you I'm better off rid of this man. You only see a side of him that he wants people to see. Privately he's so possessive.'

'Men are, but — '

'But nothing, Sheila!'

Jen tried to control her emotions, her frustrations and her desperate need for a complete break from Harris and all the shadows he left over her.

'Besides, Harris wouldn't know how to make a statement into a question like this. He flunked out of school early.'

Sheila looked taken aback by Jen's outburst and the accusation. She held out the phone, still open at the messages.

'If I was you, I would just delete

them, 'V Day' is here, and whoever he is has run out of rhyme. Leave it, delete them and then sort out Harris.'

She pushed the phone towards Jen.

'Here take it. I only want what's best for you and you don't seem to be happy on your own.'

Sheila walked off and Jen stared at the phone's display: *Delete messages? Yes/No.*

It was true, the choice was hers, but for whatever reason she did not want to rid herself of them. They might still lead to the answer to who her tormentor was — for that was what they had become, a way of tormenting her.

Jen closed her eyes and sighed.

'Miss Brightman, can I tell you something?'

Michelle's voice surprised her. Jen, feeling guilty about having her phone on in school hours jumped and accidently pressed the 'Yes' option as she squeezed the phone in her palm.

All her incoming messages were instantly deleted.

Damn! Now how could she report non-existent, non-threatening messages, even if she wanted to?

Sometimes when friends tried to help they merely made things a whole lot worse.

Jen switched the phone off.

'Michelle, you should not be here. What is it?' she asked.

'Mummy wants to talk to you soon. I . . .'

Jen glanced at her watch.

'Well, ask her to pop in after school on a Tuesday or Thursday if that's convenient and I'll see her then. If it isn't, can you ask her when would be? I can put a note in your planner in case you forget if you like. Now we must both return to the classroom.'

Jen ushered Michelle to go on ahead of her.

'Go on — you first.'

The girl nodded, deep in thought. Jen stayed a moment longer to wash her face, replacing her make-up ready to get on with the day. Perhaps the memory of the phone would be able to recall the numbers somehow.

Jen returned, avoiding any conversation at all about anything other than school-related chatter and planning — and now Sheila seemed reluctant to venture off safe ground too.

★   ★   ★

The day seemed longer than any she had ever known and when the end of the school day arrived at last, it was with relief that Jen helped the last few children on with their coats.

'I have to pop this to the office; back in five.'

Sheila raised an envelope including the sales of the tickets for the forthcoming fundraising events, and Jen saw her chance to escape before Kevin arrived.

'Here, you help Emma,' she suggested. 'I'll take that to the office.' Jen stood and held out a hand, which Sheila ignored.

'It's no problem, I'll do it,' she said, and walked out.

Jen knew that Sheila had the hump with her still. It would blow over, but she'd had such a buzz about 'V Day' and Jen knew she had been a complete wet blanket about it.

'Bye, Miss Brightman,' Michelle said when she left.

'Bye, Michelle,' Jen said, as she watched her pupil leave, noticing that Michelle was last again.

The girl had been very quiet all day. That made the day unusual too, although Jen had been too caught up in her own thoughts to realise that before now. She hoped that she was not still sulking over hearing the comments Sheila had made about her yesterday.

'Hi, Jen, is Sheila around?'

Jen turned to see Kevin standing there, bold as brass.

'If you take a seat over there, she'll be back soon; she just popped to the office.'

Jen walked into the next classroom,

knowing it was empty, but wanting to put a door or a wall — or preferably miles — between her and Kevin.

She headed for the stationery cupboard then turned to close the door behind her, but gasped as Kevin's broad frame filled the door space.

'Look, Jen . . . '

He edged inside, standing so close to her that she could smell the cologne that Sheila had bought him for her special present to him. At least he had the sense to put it on.

Other than climbing onto the shelf on which A3 coloured paper was stacked, there was nowhere for her to go and she cursed her own stupidity — she had cornered herself and she knew what he was like. The Christmas party had shown her that he had a predatory side.

'Please leave,' she warned him in a firm, but fairly quiet, voice. She certainly had no wish to be caught in a cupboard with him by Sheila — or by anyone else for that matter.

'No, Jen, listen . . . please.'

He placed a hand on her shoulder and she shrank back. He came closer and stroked her cheek with the fingers of his right hand. 'I have something for you, from Harris . . . '

'Stop there. I don't want anything from Harris. Can you please just tell him to leave me alone?'

He was so close she could feel his breath.

'You're beautiful, Jen. I never meant to scare you. I was a bit drunk and you looked divine in that little sapphire dress, complementing those lovely eyes of yours and with your hair the colour of flame. You were wearing Jo Malone for him, I knew the scent, but Harris is a simple guy. You were always wasted on him. Your perfume combined with the brandy and I just weakened, Jen. You must understand.'

'Get back or I'll scream.'

Jen was gripping a large stapler she had grabbed from the shelf. She had no idea how effective it would be, but she wanted to feel she had a weapon of some kind to protect herself with.

Kevin seemed to think for a second, his eyes looking at her lips, and then glancing at her breasts as her breath quickened. He released her shoulder and took a small step backwards.

'Your *wife* will return to the class-room in minutes, go and wait for her,' she said, emphasisng the word wife heavily.

'Wait, Jen. I have something for you,' he said and put his hand in his pocket.

'Believe me, you have nothing that I would want.'

He ignored her comment.

'Jen, ease up.'

'Me ease up? How could you come onto me when your wife was in the next room? That night we were celebrating Christmas and I was going out with your best friend and you try and hit on me! What the hell do you think I am? For that matter, what kind of man are you?' Her voice had started to rise.

Kevin stepped away from her, but

instead of leaving, he shut the cupboard door, pulling the light cord as he did so.

'Let me out!' she snapped and held the stapler tightly.

'Listen, I'd had a few. I'd also had a row with Sheila beforehand about the kids again. Can you believe it, she wanted us to have another one? We're in our forties, for heaven's sake! Anyway, I know I was wrong and I acted badly, but I really fancy you. You should be flattered. You're so . . . '

'Sweet?' Jen wondered if it was him.

He simply stared at her and looked surprised, as if he genuinely didn't know what she was talking about.

'No, well I suppose you are, but I was going to add 'so much fun', that's what I was going to say. You always see things from a fresh angle. But perhaps I should have said 'so uptight'.'

'Never mind that, just go before you're found in here with me.' Jen stared defiantly at him.

'Look, Harris left these with me to give to you. If you don't want them then return them to him any way you wish, but I said I'd get them to you and I have.'

He pulled a jewellery box out of his pocket and extended his hand to her.

Jen stared at it.

'Tell me that does not contain ruby earrings wrapped in a twisted gold thread.'

His face showed his surprise that she knew.

'Well done, Kevin. Sheila knows you have them and she thinks you're giving them to her this evening at dinner — the one you are taking her out for.'

'What? I already got her a card and chocolates. She expects jewellery as well as dinner? Bloody hell!' He rubbed his forehead. 'What do I do now?'

Jen pushed him backwards so that the door opened.

'You give them to your long suffering wife and pay Harris whatever they cost. Tell him she saw them after I had rejected them — and you can also tell him to leave me alone!'

She brushed past him and grabbed her coat as Sheila was returning down the corridor.

'Hey, just in time. Your Valentine is here. Have fun the two of you! See you in the morning, Sheila. Bye!'

Jen kept walking and didn't give Sheila the chance to speak.

She drove away from the school breathing deeply to control the shaking which had begun as she had been touched, no matter how fleetingly, by Kevin. She remembered his clumsy alcohol-fuelled moment of unbridled passion and cringed.

What a mess this week was turning out to be! One more day and it would be the weekend, however, and the messages were no more to taunt her. 'V Day', as Sheila called it, was over, the stupid presents would stop and she would be free to enjoy her life again.

She decided she would focus on planning her next venture, her summer holiday in Hong Kong. A new kind of freedom! She stopped by the shops in town and went to the travel shop. Picking up a selection of brochures on the Far East, she then returned to her apartment, where she had a date with a stack of holiday brochures, a new bottle of Merlot and a ready meal.

En route home, Jen slowed down as two policemen were just climbing into a normal looking car outside her drive. She let them go before she pulled up. What on earth were they doing there? Had she a criminal on her doorstep? Where was Mr M when she needed the gossip?

She collected up her brochures and headed for her home. Tonight in her dreams she would travel the world. How much more freedom could you have than that? Her world would open up as it had never before.

Jen saw Mr Marshall deep in conversation with someone in his bay window. The figure he was talking to was taller than him and she lingered for a moment as she locked up her Mini. She didn't like to stare. It must be the new neighbour, she reasoned. Jen wondered if she should knock on the door and ask if there was a problem. However, with her nerves raw from facing up to Kevin, and with the knowledge that Harris was seriously trying to barter for her forgiveness, she decided against it. Instead, she went to her own apartment.

Once inside, she discreetly looked out of her front window. Two figures were crossing the road, the back of the tweed jacketed Mr Marshall and the leather clad jacketed neighbour. She could not see his face clearly but knew from his build and dark hair that it was the mystery man from number two.

Whatever next? She glanced down at the bundle of brochures.

Making dreams come true, that's what!

5

Friday had arrived not a moment too soon. Her dreams had been filled with images of Hong Kong and the new Territories, of planning a train ride up to Victoria Peak with views over Hong Kong Island and Kowloon, imagining travelling to the ancient fishing village of Aberdeen and then on a sampan, or staying in a swish hotel and then exploring the famous Templar night market. All exotic, all colourful and so different that she had woken filled with excitement and a new determination to make the future her own.

The brochure prices were very expensive, but she had already done a preliminary shop around to find the cost of buying her tickets independently.

Jen locked up and stepped out onto the drive, determinedly ignoring the ominous rain clouds. Today was a new beginning she told herself.

It was with that thought that the sight that greeted her hit her harder than it should have.

The front left tyre of Jen's car was decidedly flat. She went over to it and saw what seemed to be a tack embedded in the rubber, which had obviously caused a slow puncture. When had she picked that up? Her car was no more than six weeks old — to her, anyhow. Standing there in her court shoes, long skirt, blouse and wool cardigan she did not want to start fumbling around changing the wheel for the spare. She was hardly dressed for the job and while in theory she knew how to do it, in practice she didn't know if she could remove the nuts that had last been secured by a machine.

Jen pulled out her mobile phone and began to dial a local taxi cab number.

'Problem, Jen?' Mr Marshall asked, as he strode over to her. For once he had placed his mug carefully on his window sill.

'Flat tyre, Bill. I haven't time to do it now. It will just have to wait until I get back and can change. I need to phone a taxi. I'll be so late if I don't.'

'Here,' he held out his hand toward her, 'you leave me your car keys and I'll swap your tyres and put the spare one on. Don't worry about it. It's not a problem, I assure you and I'll put the keys back in your mailbox when I'm done.'

Jen's call was answered and she turned to speak into her mobile. 'Taxi please . . . Flat One, Park Avenue. In five minutes, if possible. South Hallenton Primary school. OK. Thanks.'

Jen had heard what Mr M had offered, but felt awkward and embarrassed by it. Yet, with time ticking by her options were very limited.

'I really couldn't trouble you so much. I'll see to it when I come back . . . I . . . ' She knew her words were lame and her cheeks had flushed a deeper colour than the initial fluster had caused them to.

'Miss Brightman — Jen — I spent twenty-five years in the Royal Engineers, so I know how to change a tyre. Leave it with me and give an old fool something worthwhile to do, eh?'

He tilted his head to one side and raised an eyebrow.

'Thank you. You're very kind.'

She handed over her keys, hoping that she was right to trust him, but she listened to her intuition which told her she was.

'You are not an old fool,' she added.

He grinned. 'I know that, and you know that, but the world can be extremely judgmental of senior citizens. It forgets that our extra years of life mean years of experience too.'

She nodded in agreement.

'Good. I could run it down to the quick fix place for you — the tyre, that is, not your car — since I have to go there to change my wipers anyway. Would that be helpful?'

'More than helpful, but I don't have the cash handy to give you as I'll need some to pay the taxi.'

'I'll give you the invoice when you return and you can refund me as soon as you can. Oh, look — here's your cab. Trust me, all will be well.'

He waved to her as she climbed into the taxi.

What a start to her day!

The Friday of a week where her world seemed to have gone completely mad. Yet, her neighbour was being reliable and as she glanced at her lovely cherished car, she hoped, trustworthy.

Deciding that she would take it to a garage and have it checked out anyway over the weekend, she did not think that she was taking too big a risk.

* * *

Jen was glad to see that Sheila was happy again and back to being her usual boisterous self. Fortunately Jen's quick thinking had got her to school earlier than normal rather than later and so she had been well-prepared for the day. One which had passed moderately uneventfully.

Before long it was Friday afternoon at last and Jen entered the classroom after the children had filed back in having seen a performance by an older class in the hall. They were excited, but she had time for a story for them before home time to try and calm them down a bit.

It had been an awkward day in some ways as neither Jen nor Sheila seemed to want to mention anything to do with the recent sensitive events.

Sheila had arrived wearing her new earrings, and Jen had admired them as she would have if they had been a complete surprise to her. Sheila was obviously somewhat smug about the gift, but Jen noticed that she removed them before break and put them carefully and safely away in her purse.

They had chatted on safe subjects regarding work, but had not discussed

Harris, Kevin, roses or reconciliations again. Jen did not want to know how Sheila spent her evening with Kevin; so long as he did not come anywhere near her ever again or, friend or no friend, she would tell Sheila what he was like.

It was the fact that the couple had children that made this really awkward as she did not want to be the one who caused a family break-up. Besides, in her new frame of mind she had decided that he had made an alcohol-fuelled mistake and she had no reason to believe she wasn't the first.

It simply was just time for her to move on again.

Jen used her 'teacher's voice' and spoke across the room to all the children.

'Come along children. Story time; settle on the mat here, before home time. Sit down quietly and I will tell you a story of how dreams can sometimes come true. Jarred, no sand play now! Come on, be good.'

Thinking of her own home — yes she

liked that phrase 'own home' — she smiled as they settled into place. The day had been long and she was very tired, but knowing she had a brand new home to return to, she continued to feel the happiness her smile was trying to generate to the children.

'Once upon a time, there was a goldfish called Blinkey. He lived in a bag of water on a stall, but Blinkey dared to dream of a much grander life than that . . .'

Jen tried to put as much expression into her features as she could, opening her eyes wide, deliberately smiling as she glanced over the impressive group of youngsters in her class. This was the part of teaching she loved best. A child's imagination was a precious thing and Jen, at twenty-nine-and-three-months, was more than aware of just how much in touch she still was with her inner child.

Now with 'V Day' behind her she could dismiss the most uncomfortable week of her life; leaving Harris was not a time she would wish to repeat. The mystery phone caller had ceased to send his messages and with the others deleted by her own hand, she did not have a number to follow up.

Unless, of course, her call log held information of unanswered dialled numbers . . . perhaps she would take a look at it later.

For now she wanted these children to settle down and listen to the very short story. All stories to four and five year olds were by necessity short and fun and often carried a moral.

What a way to finish off what had been a testing, working week, Jen thought. Then, hopefully, all would be calm in the classroom before home time when the parents and carers turned up to collect them for the weekend.

Oh . . . the weekend, Jen thought, and imagined the blissful peace of it.

Back to Blinkey, she thought and made herself think fish.

'He dreamed of living in a lovely fish

tank with his best friend, the beautiful Sophie, whose bag of water rested against his own on the market stall.'

Jen saw the children smile, letting their minds fall into the fantasy.

She loved this part of her job — well most of the time. Young Emma's big smile usually lit up Jen's every morning, even though the girl struggled to do every task given to her. She tried so hard and was pleased at her every little success. A truly determinedly happy spirit, Jen had thought, as she had watched the girl struggle to hold a pen and then, over the weeks, manage to write her name. Michelle seemed to have adopted the role of Emma's mentor in order to establish one that she could accept, within the peer group.

The aspect of the job which she disliked was the paperwork that took her away from doing the actual teaching, which she so loved. Would it be too simplistic to wish she could just get on with that primary function and ditch half the forms?

At least she now had those smiles after a week of meetings, schedules, extra-curricular activities and now a dreaded Ofsted visit looming. All this on top of strange gifts, mysterious messages and facing Kevin again.

Harris was another apparently unresolved problem that she might still have to face. Not today, though, or this weekend if she could avoid it. She had to tell him to let go of her, but in doing that she would be giving him what he wanted — her attention and time. Not again.

Jen made a mental note to speak to Mr M about the stranger who seemed to stalk the alleyway and claimed to be her neighbour at number two. Funny how she didn't trust what anyone told her any more.

'I dream a lot,' Michelle stated brightly, copying Jen's mannerisms; she had widened her eyes also and peered around the group. Sheila was helping in the hall before returning to tidy up, and Jen noticed how relaxed Michelle was again. The girl really should learn not to eavesdrop — you don't always hear what you want to know — but she was only a curious child.

Michelle was sitting among the other children at the far side of the story circle to Jen, on the edge of the story-time mat. Some of the other children nodded and started to whisper to each other.

Jen could see that Michelle liked her new feeling of power as she continued, 'I dream of dragons and a shiny, silvery egg. Not gold like the goose's one, but silver. It made magic too . . . '

'Sh!' Jen interrupted rather abruptly, seeing a stronger and more gripping story opening up from her young competitor. How could Blinkey compare to Michelle's silver, musical, egg-laying dragon?

'Listen to the story, Michelle,' Jen said, trying to keep her voice light and making her lips smile. She admired the girl's ability. She was full of character, bright as could be. It was as though she thought herself above the other children, but in a matter-of-fact way, rather than in an arrogant way. Her frustration with the slower children made her a handful to keep occupied as she constantly sought attention and to be challenged. Jen often wondered why this was so, but had not seen her parents as she was dropped off and picked up by her gran.

Jen paused momentarily, as she glanced around the small group of children seated before her and waited until they all looked back at her. Peace she thought, at last they were listening; she loved it when they hung on the next word of a story and were completely lost to it. A child's mind was a power to behold — beautiful if nurtured creatively.

Michelle's mouth had fallen into a slight sulk as she started to twizzle her hair around her fingers. So she can be childish, too, Jen thought. It reassured her and she continued with the story leaving Michelle to her own devices.

'Blinkey's dream was quite simple; he wanted to be able to swim with his friend Sophie in their own tank. To Blinkey this would be bliss . . . ' Jen cringed a little. She had meant to change that word when she wrote the story, but had forgotten to. Bliss was an old fashioned term. It was how she had thought of her apartment, her space, her peace — her bliss!

'What's bliss, miss?' asked Michelle.

Jen smiled as she answered, realising that Michelle would pick up on it straight away.

'Bliss is when you feel you are very, very happy,' she said and wished she could say it was what she felt right now.

Jen continued, 'Early one morning, the circus was just beginning to set up its stalls. Blinkey looked at the shelf where he would be put on show, in his own little bag filled with fresh water and — '

'Miss Brightman!'

'Yes, Michelle,' Jen answered, seeing some of the other younger children like

126

Jarred becoming distracted. His concentration was about to wander back to the sand pit where he had been happily playing before she had insisted it was story time. Sheila had returned and was quietly replacing various toys and equipment on their allotted shelf spaces, all clearly marked out by area: pans in the kitchen, books in the library, scoops and pots in the sand play area and so on until the room was tidy and ready for the weekend.

'Can goldfish blink?' the girl asked absentmindedly, watching Sheila as she placed the items back on the shelf space, while she continued curling a long strand of her mousy blonde hair around her fingers in one hand and pulling at the bow on her shoe with the other.

'Michelle, you need to be quiet and listen to the story, or else you won't be able to understand what is happening and will spoil the enjoyment for the other children.'

Jen fixed the girl with what she hoped

was a firm, no nonsense warning stare.

'It's just a story, and just as dogs can't really talk, in stories they often can.' She smiled, and Michelle nodded. 'No, goldfish can't really blink. Now, back to the story,' Jen said firmly and continued with, 'Blinkey was a happy fish most days . . .'

'Don't know why. If I was in a bag of water ready to be put on a shelf, I wouldn't be happy if that was how my day began,' Michelle mumbled. 'Stupid fish!'

'Michelle, stand up and go and sit in the corner on your own until you can behave yourself.'

The girl stomped over to the naughty stool, where she could focus undisturbed on her locks and her bow.

Jen smiled at the other children reassuringly, annoyed that what had been intended to be a simple short story designed to fill in ten minutes at the end of a long day, and an ever longer week, had been so interrupted.

Still, Jen's new flat awaited, a glass of

wine was ready in her new wine rack by the fridge, with her pasta dinner ready to warm up as soon as she arrived and then an evening all to herself.

No more Harris, no more messages and no more trying to feel at home in someone else's house. No more of Harris trying to control her life. She had achieved her dream; she had her own bowl to swim in now — happily and blissfully alone.

'Blinkey happily flicked his fin and swam together with Sophie in their very own tank,' she finished after a few minutes and Jen's smile was genuine as she too felt the freedom to do as she wanted. Last year had been a very long and unhappy year, but not this one, this one was going to be just great.

'Need the toilet, miss!' Jarred said and his hand shot up in the air.

'Be quick then.' She let him go. It was no use, some days they just wore her energy down. No, that was unfair. The children usually filled her with ideas and fun, it was all the preamble to

'V Day' which had undermined her new found confidence. Her job had kept her sane throughout the relationship with Harris, for here Jen was in control.

Determinedly, she wound up the story, whilst the two biggest detractors were occupied. Reading out the last line whilst withholding a sigh of relief, she announced that, 'Blinkey blinked, because dreams sometimes can come true.'

The children left seemed to have enjoyed the happy ending and hopefully absorbed some of the message of the story that you should not give up just because something seems difficult. Emma knew this already and Jen was so glad of that.

'Now, children, get your coats from . . .'

Well there was no need to finish that sentence as they raced out toward their coat hooks. Instead, Jen released Michelle from her penance on the naughty stool.

'Apology?' Jen said, as the girl looked up impishly at her.

'Sorry,' she muttered. 'Miss Bright-man, what do you dream about?' Michelle asked, her eyes seeming to show a genuine and keen curiosity.

'Why don't you tell me what you dream about?'

Jen turned the question around not wanting to explain anything of her own dreams to this near six year old who had intelligence beyond her years. She was also aware that Sheila had looked across and raised an eyebrow at her. Jen did not want to be accused of favouritism, so was careful not to become too familiar by answering her question.

'I dream of telling stories. I dream of a dragon who laid a silver egg with a magic, musical, message that only a good child could know and I dream I am that child.'

The girl stared at Jen and then coloured slightly.

'Then on Monday, Michelle, you can tell me that story and, if it is as good as you think it is, then I will let you tell the

131

class it at story-time.'

Michelle jumped up and hugged Jen, which really took her by surprise, and she whispered, 'I do love my mummy,' before she ran from the classroom, shouting back, 'It is a good story, really!' as she grabbed her coat off the hook and continued towards her grandmother who waited for her at the doorway of the school.

Jen shook her head. Why on earth had the child made such a declaration to her? Strange, she thought, but she smiled as it dawned on Jen that she had, apparently, the power to grant a girl's dreams too. Michelle may yet have her turn at story telling.

She went to find Jarred, who had taken his time as usual, not having returned from the children's bathroom. As she looked over the line of small cubicles, Jen often thought it was like going into the land of Lilliput. She found Jarred transfixed, bending over staring into the white bowl of the toilet, the cubicle door wide open.

'What's wrong, Jarred?' she asked, bracing herself for some piece of information she really did not want to hear.

He pointed into the bowl. 'It's Blinkey, Miss. He's swimming without his bag.'

Jen's heart skipped a beat as she visualised the tank of fish in the corridor just outside the classroom. There were two ways in and out of the toilets: one from the class room and the other from the corridor. Anxiously, she looked into the bowl and saw one of the plastic fish from the sand play corner floating on top of the water and she gulped with relief.

'That was a silly thing to do, Jarred. No sand playing for you next week. The boy looked slightly dejected as he realised this meant he would be sitting on a stool whilst others played for a lesson and his bottom lip protruded.

'Go and get your coat.'

The boy slumped off as Jen tried to flush the toy away, but alas, it would not go, so she looked around for something to scoop up the plastic fish from the toilet to put it straight into the bin. She had to smile at the idea, though, that he had thought he had set Blinkey free. Whatever would he do with one of his mum's eggs after hearing Michelle's story?

Fortunately, Sheila was seeing to the handover of the children to their parents, whilst Jen was tied up.

With blue rubber gloves on her hands and sporting a pair of tongs she used for messy jobs such as when they were dyeing anything, she was crossing the now empty classroom when a voice cut into her thoughts.

'Hello.'

Jen stopped mid walk, startled by the appearance of a quiet, but handsome man wearing a black bomber-style jacket. There was something familiar about him that she could not quite place.

'Can I help you?' she asked.

'Yes, I'm looking for the teacher,' he

said abstractedly. 'I was told she was in here. Did I miss her?'

Jen had had a tiring day at the end of a very demanding week and was about to round on this good looking, seemingly charming man, but then she became embarrassingly aware of her appearance, sporting rubber gloves and tongs.

'Well depending on which teacher you are seeking, you might have found her.' She pulled off the gloves.

He glanced at her, smiling in a familiar way, then did a double take as he recognised her.

'Miss Jennifer Brightman? Jen?'

'Yes, that's me and you are?'

Jen was wracking her brains to try and pair him to one of her pupils, but there was not a hint of similarity to any of the youngsters that instantly struck her; or perhaps it was more a case that for some surprising reason she did not want him to be the father of one. He must have been roughly the same age as her, late twenties or perhaps early thirties.

Realisation dawned. He looked like a security man and she had met him in the alleyway by her apartment door. In fact she had introduced herself as Jen — he was the stranger from number two. Instantly, she was filled with a feeling of alarm. He was here in her classroom. How did he know where to find her? Why was he in the school building? Her grip on the tongs tightened.

'I'm Sergeant Lee,' he said. 'We met once before, near my flat. I came here directly because I thought — '

'Sergeant? You're a policeman?'

It took a second for her to grasp that he was actually a policeman, which was why he came and went at odd hours and police cars were appearing at odd times along Park Avenue. Not the hoodlums causing concern as Mr Marshall had presumed, although that would explain why he had walked off with him into the park.

The next word that came into her

mind was 'trouble'. A flat tyre did not warrant a visit from the police, unless something had happened to Mr Marshall and/or her Mini. Her mind spun with possibilities. Who had done what, now?

'Has something else happened?' Jen asked, casually dropping the gloves and tongs on to a table as Sheila returned to the room looking more than a little curiously at the good looking stranger who was engaged in what appeared to be becoming an intense conversation with Jen.

'I just wanted to give you an update on the situation seeing as . . . ' He hesitated as Sheila arrived. ' . . . since I was passing. I've just been to the scene of the break-in and was told by your neighbour that you work here. I thought I would get the details to you directly, as we're based just up the road and I was familiar with the address. I've arranged for CSI to do prints and so on.'

He was starting to slow the pace of

his conversation down as Jen stared back at him with a completely shocked expression, then leaned against the table she had been standing in front of.

'There's something else?' Sergeant Lee asked.

'Her day started off badly with a flat tyre,' Sheila tried to explain, whilst Jen gathered her thoughts together.

Jen had a mental image of appearing like 'Blinkey' the dumb fish, only this dream was rapidly becoming another nightmare.

'A break-in . . . ?'

Images of petals, messages, a bottle of wine, flowers, a tack . . . now a break-in. Was she going completely mad or had someone got it in for her? How much was coincidence and how much not? Now her neighbour, the shadowy figure who came and went at odd hours was standing before her. A policeman . . . of course she had seen a police car drive off . . . of course he wore heavy black boots . . . he was the police.

Jen's head was starting to spin. She

felt as though she had missed an important announcement. Why would he be there for her? It made no sense to her at all and why would he be talking about CSI — like they do on TV?

Judy, the young office assistant turned up. She was a temp from the agency who was covering for maternity leave.

They all missed Cheryl and her annoying OCD ways of pestering them for details, but she had done a better job than anyone had ever given her credit for. Now they were into crisis and anger management with a frustrated head teacher to contend with as a result, and parents' complaints as they were placed on hold for too long.

'Hi . . . ' Judy rushed in.

She smiled sweetly at the policeman, who tactfully nodded.

'I'm so glad, I caught you, Jenny. Mr Marshall, your neighbour, phoned. He left a message to say could you phone him as soon as you can? He said he wouldn't normally bother you at school but he had to this time. So could you give him a ring now?'

Judy handed Jen a piece of paper with her neighbour's number written on it.

'When did this message arrive?' Jen asked, and saw that Sergeant Lee looked rather awkward as he shifted his weight to the other foot. She could see his handsome features clearly now. No menace as the half shadowed encounter previously had cast. He had very dark brown eyes and strong lashes.

'Oh. It must have been about 2p.m., possibly half past,' she said and smiled, still glancing at Lee.

'Why have you only just told me this now, if it was urgent? You should have told me straight away!' Jen snapped at her.

Judy looked taken aback. 'Well, class has finished now! Private phone calls aren't allowed during the class times, Mr Finch said.'

Judy folded her arms, and continued to smile furtively at their visitor.

'Unless it's something *urgent*,' Jen added, glaring at the girl. 'And I'm Miss Brightman or Jen. Please don't call me Jenny.'

Judy seemed to have had enough sense to realise her mistake even if she was not going to admit to it, or apologise.

'Well, let's hope it isn't that urgent then,' she quipped. 'Must dash. Got to finish up before I can go home.'

She looked to Sheila and then the stranger.

'Bye!' She wiggled her fingers in a gesture of a wave and left them staring at each other.

Jen looked at her neighbour — her stranger — bearer of more bad news.

'So tell me exactly how urgent is it, Sergeant?'

She was half sitting on one of the tables, using it as a prop really, as he began to explain to her what had happened.

6

Do you have a car here or any mode of transport, Miss Brightman?' Sergeant Lee asked.

Jen stared blankly back at him. She had a strong feeling he already knew the situation regarding her tyre and that was why he had turned up at the school. She also suspected that the suggestion may even have come from Mr Marshall. The two of them were obviously acquainted and, as she had not responded to the urgent phone call, it did seem very likely that Mr M had raised the alarm further.

Jen hoped that her neighbour had not been hurt in whatever had happened at her home. The word 'burglary' was running through her brain, followed by the phrases 'break-in' and 'back door'. She thought that the UPVC door was secured with its five dead bolts, but Jen couldn't quite get her mind around what was happening. She was vaguely aware of Sheila's hand on her back, giving off feelings of comfort, reassurance and possibly even pity for this latest bit of bad news.

'If you do . . . so long as you feel OK to drive, that is,' Sergeant Lee went on, 'I'll follow you back down the coast road to your apartment.' He was staring at her as if trying to decide if she was taking in what he was saying or not. 'But if you haven't, then I can give you a lift there now.'

Jen was unaware of being silent as she looked back into his eyes . . . deep dark brown pools, she thought. They reminded her of something, a picture or a place she had looked on recently, but she couldn't put her finger on the image she was trying to remember.

Everything was topsy-turvy in her world at that moment, or more precisely, nothing seemed as it should be anymore. She was lost to what his words were asking as a mixture of tiredness and shock muffled her senses further.

Jen felt as if she could literally swoon, just fall forward and drift off to some other plain, but then, as she felt Sheila prod her gently in the back, the world came back into focus. She straightened up and concentrated her attention on what was happening around her. Reality returned and she smiled quickly, if a little insincerely, at him.

'No . . . No, I don't, well not today. I normally do, but I had a flat so had to take a taxi this morning to get in on time. So, thank you, I would be glad of a lift. If you don't mind?'

Jen pulled on her coat and picked up her bags, knowing that her apartment was not exactly out of his way. Neither was she leaving the classroom as she would have wished to, but now was not a time to fuss about such things.

'Of course I don't, it's no problem. I'll meet you outside.'

He pressed a button on his small walkie-talkie device, spoke into it as he unclipped it from his jacket pocket and strolled away, still chatting into it.

Jen watched him. No wonder he was a mystery to her, a man who kept odd hours.

'You OK, Jen?' Sheila asked. 'I can come down later on if you like. I have to pick up Hailey first, though, but I could leave her at my mum's place if you want, for a few hours anyway, she would understand.'

She looked so concerned that Jen felt almost guilty for causing her any need to feel so bad.

When Jen didn't respond instantly, Sheila continued, 'Try not to panic, Jen. It might not be as awful as it sounds . . . or could sound, that is.' She tried to make a reassuring smile and gesture, but it was not coming across that way. 'I could get Kevin to pop around later and see if he can fix anything up for you. He's so good with his hands.'

Jen stared at her blankly and swallowed.

'Kevin and Harris are handy guys to have around and . . . '

Her words drifted off as Jen stepped away from her, unable to hide the horror she felt that, on top of what she now must face, Sheila was suggesting bringing in the two people she least wanted to see in her world.

'I'll be fine. It can't be that bad or they wouldn't have waited for me to finish teaching before sending out the troops, would they?' Jen asked, seeking a little bit of reassurance.

At the same time she felt like going around to the office to give Judy a piece of her mind about what she should consider as 'urgent' in future — like a home being violated — but then she knew it would be unfair as the girl had a lot to learn yet, this being her first week.

'Oh, the plastic fish — Jarred!' Jen suddenly remembered what she had been doing.

'I'll see to it, Jen,' Sheila offered. 'You go on home.'

Jen nodded her thanks.

'Sheila, please don't involve Kevin or Harris in this. This is my problem to sort out. You just enjoy your weekend and I'll be fine. I have friends who can help me and Kevin should be spending time with you and . . . well, I don't mean to be rude but . . . well, please don't mention Harris again. He wouldn't be any help at all. He would just try to take over my life again and I won't let him. Sheila, you really don't know him as I do.'

Sheila nodded, though reluctantly.

'As you wish, Jen. I just thought . . . '

'Thanks,' Jen said. 'I know you meant well and you're only trying to help.'

Jen was also aware that her neighbour, Mr Marshall, would be worried about it all and her; he was old fashioned in his ways, not really understanding why a young woman would want to live on her own.

As a widower, loneliness was something he had told her he loathed, so his cure was to keep busy and do things, then his world would keep turning. It was an attitude she liked and found inspirational. He was not a young man, but he was active and quite fit, and the fact that he might be caught up in this mess disturbed her deeply. Her thoughts had drifted off as if she were trying to blank the panicked realisation of where she was and what was happening.

'Well, promise you'll phone me later,' Sheila shouted from the doorway of the school, looking, Jen thought, a little relieved that she had been excused. 'If you need somewhere to kip tonight, you can always stay at mine. We have a sofa bed and you're always welcome.'

She stepped outside a few yards and gave Jen a hug.

'Thanks,' Jen said a little awkwardly. The last thing she wanted to do now was become emotional, so instead she smiled as confidently as she could and promised she would call her friend as soon as she herself knew what was happening.

'There'll be things to sort out so it might be later in the evening before I get the chance.'

Sheila nodded. 'OK, and don't worry, I'll finish up here. See you Monday.'

Jen knew it would be much later in the day when she phoned Sheila because Kevin would be at the gym from nine. It was Friday and he and Harris always met down there at the end of the week. So Jen would phone Sheila when she knew that Kevin would be out and her friend would definitely pick up her call.

⋆　⋆　⋆

Beneath Jen's bold external shell, she was starting to shake as she sat in the police car. Under different circumstances her inner child would have been quite excited at the prospect of it, but like this, she was filled with dread.

Jen was devastated, but was trying, and failing, not to show it. Her ideal week had turned out to be a complete disaster from Monday onwards. She had nervously taken her place in the front passenger seat. Aware that there were still enough people around the school for curious eyes to take note of this unusual departure, she knew that she would be the talk of the staff room and amongst the cleaners next week. She didn't want their pity, she didn't want attention, all she wanted was to be allowed to live her life undisturbed. Was that too much to expect?

The caretaker, who just happened to be crossing the car park, was waiting to lock the gates for the weekend once the cars had all left. He looked at her and waved sympathetically. She was sure that the classroom was bugged sometimes — how else did word spread so fast? Then she shook her head dismissively. More paranoia.

Lee would have had to go to the office first and see Mr Finch, who would have phoned through to George the caretaker so that he knew why there was a police car in the car park. It was so obvious, yet she was ready to believe that gossip was rife.

'Are you OK, Miss Brightman?' Sergeant Lee asked as he climbed in alongside her, looking at her curiously.

'Yes, I'm fine. Are you not allowed to call me Jen, as a neighbour?' she asked, trying to divert his attention and attempt a normal conversation, in a world where her 'normality' seemed to have gone on vacation.

He smiled at her. 'I can call you whatever name you're comfortable with me using.'

'Then please call me Jen. I could do with feeling as if I'm with a friend right now.'

Jen had gone with Sergeant Lee happily enough, grateful she was not having to summon another taxi or get on a bus on her own, lost in her own unpredictable thoughts whilst stifling an urge to scream and rant and rave at the unfairness of it all. Goodness only knows where she would have ended up if she had had to use public transport today!

Her mind had turned to mush again, her inner child feeling frightened and also angry that someone had singled her out for this act of vandalism.

She had shared Michelle's joy and enthusiasm for leaving school with something to look forward to. Michelle had established a place of her own within the class that she had so recently joined, and now had her own story to write. Jen had established her own home, but someone had spoilt it before she'd had a chance to truly experience the joy of it for herself.

This was the first weekend she was not unpacking her belongings or cleaning. Only on Monday she'd said that she was in her own apartment and was so happy. Her space had been as she wished it. Thinking back to her awful nightmare she wondered why fate had decreed that she now had to live out a new nightmare.

Glancing at the defined features of

the man next to her; his dark, almost black hair, so neat that it emphasised his lovely tanned complexion, she thought that it had not been attained in Ebton. Jen was glad she would be going back to her home with someone able and used to dealing with this sort of thing; the sort of thing that had never before touched her life.

How fortunate she had been in life until now, she realised. Despite Harris and his controlling ways, she had never come across real criminals before or felt threatened or violated.

'Excuse me; I must phone Mr Marshall, our neighbour,' she said, thinking about how the old man might be worried.

'Go ahead. He's a nice enough chap. It was him who called me and told me about your door.'

Jen dialled Mr Marshall's number and waited for him to pick up. She wanted to reassure him that all would now be sorted out — and in so doing she hoped to reassure herself — and she wanted to thank him for seeing to her car. If he hadn't, it could have been damaged too.

'Hello, Mr Marshall . . . Yes, I've just been told about it . . . Yes, I know that, but school rules, I'm afraid . . . No, I'm fine. Yes, Sergeant Lee is here. He's driving me back now in fact. I'm on my way now . . . Absolutely not! If you hadn't been at the tyre centre when this happened, then you could have been hurt yourself and if the keys had been put through the door earlier then I could have lost my Mini. You did me a double favour.'

Jen paused, realising that her conversation might in some way being monitored or assessed by the policeman. Jen wondered if they were ever truly off duty, or whether they went around observing and watching the world as their training had taught them to be ever vigilant. Or perhaps she had watched too many TV detective series.

'Mr M — sorry, Bill — if you had disturbed them, whoever they were, you might be in hospital now,' she went on, reassuring her neighbour's concerns. 'So I'm really glad you weren't there, but thank you again for being so vigilant and noticing the apartment had been broken into and reporting it . . . Yes, that's right, I'm with Sergeant Lee right now . . . No I hadn't, small world. I really must go now. See you soon. Thanks. Bye.'

She replaced her mobile phone in her bag.

Jen sat there, anxious and amazed that this disturbing week was ending in such a dramatic fashion, with a lift in a police car to her own home — now apparently a crime scene.

Suddenly her previous dilemmas of paperwork and plastic fish down toilet bowls faded into oblivion, but the doubts over a connection between the unwanted surprise gifts and those messages, the tyre, and now this, continued to linger.

She needed to talk with Sergeant Lee about them all, but without sounding quite as neurotic as she currently felt. Her desire to cry was strong, but that was not what she was normally like. Perhaps now was not the time to pour out her fears. When she knew what it was she was dealing with today, then perhaps she would explain further to the Sergeant.

'You've been there already and seen it.' She looked at the officer, trying to judge from the man's body language his true reaction to her question. 'How bad is it?' she asked, as much to break the silence as to find out the information.

Bizzarely she noticed that he had straight eyelashes, which when seen from the side view were quite long.

He kept his focus upon the road, but glanced at her quickly as he replied, 'I apologise for not making sure you were aware of the situation first, before I started talking to you about it. Are you sure you're alright?' he asked, then paused before adding, 'It's normal to feel a bit shaken at such a piece of news. I should have checked you'd been given the message before bursting in with it, but I'd hoped to catch you before you left since I knew that William had seen to your car tyre.'

'William?'

'Mr Marshall,' he answered.

'Yes, of course, Bill,' she said puzzled.

'Yes, Bill. Sorry, William's the name I've known him by for many years. Jen, do you have a friend or a partner, someone you'd like to call?' he asked casually.

'No, I've not lived there for long and I live on my own.'

She thought for a moment. He might already know this. If he had spoken to Mr M and they were old friends she was sure the fact that they were the only two inhabitants of the new flats would have cropped up and also that she was the other owner.

Yes, she lived on her own, and had been so happy about that fact, but now someone else had been in there and knew where she kept all her things, from private nick-knacks to her under-wear — how incredibly vulnerable that made her feel.

'I don't want to cause upset or concern to anyone else. How bad is it?' She repeated her question, not sure if he had heard her the first time, although he gave the impression of being a very perceptive person.

'The bottom panel of the kitchen door has been forced open and inside the contents of drawers and cupboards have been thrown over the floor and furniture, so it looks a bit of a mess, but it doesn't seem as if there's been any malicious breakages or damage done.'

He paused, while he manoeuvred around a roundabout, or perhaps to let this information sink in before adding more.

'Except for a broken back door and a clear disregard for other people's property,' Jen said angrily, but it was as much to cover up the horrible fear and growing sense of violation that was developing within her. She had never had anything personal stolen before, let alone to have someone go through her home, her own treasured space, and take her private belongings.

'That door was supposed to be a security feature. It has five-lever something or other that secures it all around! I believed it would hold fast,' Jen said quite angrily.

'Yes, it did and they do. You could say it did its job in that way, but the weakness in these doors is that the bottom panels below the glass ones can be levered open quite quickly with a bit of force — all a person needs is to be agile enough to climb through the over-sized cat-flap it effectively makes.'

Jen felt like a fool who had fallen for a sales pitch and had been taken as gullible by the estate agent who had shown her the special 'features'.

Her mind was instantly filled with lists: things that would be of any value — they would make up the shortest list; next her list of things of a sentimental value — this would form a much longer one; then a list of financial and legal documents like passport, driving licence, credit card details and so on. Then the lists crossed over, with those things that were both sentimental and valuable. This would not be easy to sort out.

Jen was suddenly hit by a new wave of concern. She thought about her new passport, which she had only recently received, and had not even had the chance to use yet. She was oblivious to what he was saying as a new fear grew within her: what if her identity was being stolen as she was sitting there?

Jen had read a thriller novel about such a thing. Could it really happen to her? She had read somewhere that identity theft was on the rise and with that thought her fear began to grow again. She breathed deeply and tried to fight back the feeling of growing panic consuming her — along with the desire to cry her heart out. All she had wanted was a place of her own, to be left to enjoy it, while she decided what she was going to do next in her life — her holiday, the much needed break and adventure.

Her mind ran on freely with more ideas and more questions leading to a new wave of mounting anger, mixed with more than a little bit of the fear at the intimidation she had felt this week. Then there was the sinking feeling that she might not be safe living there anymore. Her new home, her new independent space. What if the thieves returned? Where else could she go to live? Her parents lived in the Isle of Wight.

A picture of Harris holding his arms out to her before he fell upon her in her nightmare appeared to her as large as life; it hovered in her mind like an angel of death. No, she would never go back to him.

'Miss Brightman . . . Miss Brightman . . . Jen!' Lee snapped her name out, seemingly to get her attention, and it worked.

'Sorry!' she blurted out as his words

finally penetrated her subconscious.

'You seemed very distracted. Are you certain you can't phone for a friend to meet us there?' he repeated. 'You're looking quite pale actually and I'd like to make sure you're not in shock.'

She laughed; it escaped her on a wave of nervous anxiety, almost like a kind of release.

'I'm afraid that's a consequence of my colouring, being auburn.' She never liked to be called ginger. 'I tend to be pale at the best of times. I'm fine, just lost in thought, that's all.'

She managed to smile and was surprised that her voice had not wavered once.

'We'll be there soon,' he said reassuringly. 'Try to stay calm. It really isn't as bad a scene as it could be, as far as burglaries go, that is.'

Jen was quite touched that he showed such concern, because his words had been spoken in a genuine manner. His job was to deal with the darker side of life. Daily he would face the violators

162

and their victims, yet he seemed empathetic rather than cynical. How could she explain to him that she was a dreamer, and had had a vivid imagination all her life, which at times like this turned a bad situation into a complete nightmare? Or that that same imagination had been severely tested through the whole of this week.

Taking reality on the chin was hard enough; adding onto it the extra possibilities in her thoughts turned the reality of these strange happenings into major instances of menace. What had appeared to be an isolated incident, possibly an opportunist seeking a quick grab of goodies, had turned into a full length thriller of stalking, intimidation and loss of her identity.

Mayhem and intrigue began to fill her mind again. Suddenly, getting to grips with the kids in the classroom seemed like a walk in the park — but as Michelle had told her even that was not safe. Yet she had looked forward to relaxing in her flat, chilling out for a weekend and planning her next great adventure. Jen was at the start on a life-changing plan, daring herself to try something new and very different; every month she would make herself enter into a new experience.

First, she had made the split from a bully, then the car had been purchased — one which was completely of her choice, her dream fulfilled to own a new Mini — then the major move into her own flat, with her own choice of décor.

Now she had another new experience to add to these, that of a burglary. That one had not been on her list.

This month's challenge had been to swot up on her journey to the Far East — this time she was going for exotic. However, dealing with a broken down door was not what she had planned to spend her weekend grappling with. She had moved away from one mistake — a year-long one called Harris — leaving the hurt behind, and had started anew, and here she was having to deal with a possibly trashed flat. That hurt — it hurt deeply!

'Miss Brightman?' Lee said and side-glanced at her again.

'Sorry. I really am fine. Honestly, I am. It's just that I have a very good imagination, which I think may be making things a lot worse for me than they might actually be.'

'Try not to make it personal. These things rarely are to the perpetrator, but of course to their victims, it all appears so because it's such an intrusion.'

Jen stared out of the window as they moved ever closer to having to face her fears. They drove alongside the park opposite and she stared absently into it. Normally, she just glanced that way as she drove along. Now in order to gather her senses and calm her emotions she actually looked through the fence at the people inside.

There was the man from further down the road with his Airedale terrier throwing a ball as he played with it on the open stretch of grass. Two teenagers were kicking a ball around at the other end of the green and then there was the girl feeding bread to the ducks with her grandmother . . .

'Michelle!' she said, voicing the name out loud as she realised who it was that she was watching.

'Pardon?' Sergeant Lee asked her to explain the sudden outburst of a name.

'Sorry, I was just surprised to see one of the girls from my class here. I mean, our catchment area doesn't extend this far.'

'Come to play in the park, no doubt,' he said simply.

'Yes, of course.'

She continued to watch the girl and her grandmother laugh and play together. The woman was fitter and younger than Jen had imagined from the distant image that had been created as she collected Michelle from school.

The car continued along towards what was in fact their shared drive.

Jen remembered that Michelle had said that her mum had wanted to speak to her. She wondered why, and if it was something to do with Michelle, or if it was more personal; perhaps it was something to do with what had been happening at her flat. Had they seen something, did the woman know something about who left the petals or the bottle of wine? Or had her imagination just gone off down a new direction again. Why would a stranger think there was anything odd about something being delivered.

Lee turned the car into the drive and parked it behind her Mini. She was so relieved that the tyre was indeed fixed and her car was untouched.

'You will come in with me, won't you?' she asked him, hoping she did not sound like a total wimp, but also hoping he was not going to simply drop her at the scene then just walk away. She did not look back at him, but instead stared out at the apartment block.

He smiled at her when she asked that and although Jen missed it, she could hear humour within his voice.

'I thought it might help you if I did. They don't tend to approve of us just acting as a taxi service,' he said gently.

'Sorry, I wasn't thinking right.'

She continued to stare out of the side window.

'As we go in, try not to touch anything. I'll need to know if anything major is missing and just get a few basic questions answered, like, do you smoke?'

Her head spun around. If he was trying to change the subject this was one way of doing it which she did not expect.

'No, I don't like the things. I'm afraid that having one would not steady my nerves. It would only make me cough.'

She looked at him with a surprised expression.

He took his attention off her for the briefest of moments and was unable to stifle a laugh. A big grin lit up his face as he looked back at her.

'I wasn't offering you one, Jen.' He regained his businesslike composure and began to explain. 'I apologise for laughing. I asked because, when we first entered, I found a discarded cigarette wrapper on the carpet in one of the rooms and we wondered if it was yours.'

He returned his full attention to her as he spoke.

'Oh, I see.'

She flushed slightly, giving her face some colour. She had to get a grip on reality, she obviously was not thinking straight.

'No, I don't and I wouldn't drop a wrapper of any sort on my own carpet. I have bins for that sort of thing.'

She thought of someone smoking in her home, defiling her carpet and wondered what else they had done to it.

'It was on the bedroom carpet. Would anyone you know have left it there? We need to be able to analyse it — if it's definitely the burglar's then it could possibly give us a clear identification if he or she already has a record.'

'I don't know anyone who would leave such a thing in my bedroom.

No-one else has been in there to my knowledge. No, it must be his or hers.'

The thought that the burglar could be a woman struck Jen as odd, but then there was no reason why it could not be, she supposed. Desperate people must come in both sexes and in Jen's mind anyone who had to resort to destroying the life or property of anyone else must be desperate — or desperately lacking in some basic humanity.

Lee nodded.

'Then we may just be lucky. That will be the first piece of possible evidence which we will leave alone for the CSI team to look at. Now, brace yourself for the shock of seeing your home in a bit of a mess.'

7

They had pulled up outside the modern development of four one and two bedroomed maisonettes, one up one down, forming a block on the main road into town opposite Lake Park. The houses either side of her block were larger pre-war, detached, solid brick builds which continued lining the side of the road into town.

The curtain of Mr Marshall's front window in the house next door moved open as he clearly had been waiting to see them return. He raised a hand in the air to acknowledge their arrival.

'Do you know him well?' she asked.

Sergeant Lee casually acknowledged Mr M with a raised hand and a gentle wave. Lee opened the car door wide and held it for her. She thought that was such a sweet and old-fashioned thing to do, but he seemed perfectly at ease with it.

'Yes,' was the brief reply he made. 'I do know him.'

Jen walked to the alleyway. She was surprised that Mr Marshall had not appeared. Jen had waved back at him as she stepped out of the car, making herself smile politely as if to reassure him all would be well. It was strange really, because it was she who was definitely in need of some comfort and reassurance. He had waved back and seemed happy to leave her in the hands of the law. Perhaps he would pop round later.

Sergeant Lee waited for Jen at the side gate.

'It's the personal intrusion that usually takes time getting over,' he said, and then continued down the small passageway that led to both her back door and his own, facing onto the garden area at the back.

Jen followed him to the broken door that led her into the ground floor flat.

She had intended it to remain hers for at least the next couple of years. Then she had hoped to decide whether to stay in the area or move on. She had the option of renting it out or selling it if the market was favourable.

Either way she was trying to build up enough courage to venture further out into the world. Right now, moving on seemed like an excellent idea, but perhaps that was the coward in her talking, for home had suddenly become more daunting than working in foreign lands perhaps.

Somewhere exotic was what Jen was planning; a holiday first to see if she liked it and then — who knew? Harris had repeatedly told her that she was a pussycat in hiding beneath a tiger's skin. This was, she had realised rather late, his charmingly indelicate way of undermining her self confidence; he of course, considered himself to be the complete reverse.

Lee stopped by the back door.

'Our kindly neighbour has balanced a

piece of board against it as a weather guard.'

He glanced up at the sun which was still shining although lacking much heat as it was still too early for springtime.

'You'll have to get someone to come and secure it properly for you. I've called the Crime Scene people. They'll be here later to do the prints and so on. Perhaps you could organise someone to do it for you after they've been.'

He spoke to her as he continued moving the board away so that the door could be opened.

Jen looked at the UPVC door. She was stunned. The door was secure, as in the secure lock and bolts still held it firmly in place, which was what she had been promised would happen, but the lower panel had been prised open so that it now resembled a giant cat flap.

'So much for the extra bolts and things on the locks. The estate agent had gone to lengths to point out to me that was a security feature of the build,' she said, and looked at the mess beyond it when she unlocked the door's remains so they could enter. After all, she was a young woman living on her own in a ground floor flat so safety had seemed so very important to her. Whoever had broken in had just levered the lower panel open and simply climbed through. She pushed it open.

'To be honest, I would replace it with a solid glass one,' Lee suggested. 'It puts them off — security glass is a deterrent, it takes a lot of force to break through it, making a helluva lot of noise, and smashes into lots of pieces, so there's a greater chance of them being heard or injured in the process of breaking in. So for the 'hit and run' type of burglary, penetrating such a door simply is not worth their effort. Mind you, that isn't an official recommendation,' he added a little sheepishly, 'just a thought as you'll have to see to getting a new one. Wood works well too; it is very hard to break through and splinters easily.'

Jen stepped inside. The kitchen

diner was almost part of the living room with only an open doorway dividing the two areas. The whole floor was littered with the contents of her desk drawers and things from the oak unit she had placed lovingly in the corner. The matching oak flooring acted like a background to this abstract art display of personal belongings and homely nicknacks. There was a tumble of items thrown haphazardly over the chairs, but they were her own things.

'Why do they have to make such a mess?' Jen asked, as she just stared at it all.

'This way they don't have to touch much and can easily see what is there by just picking out the things they want. It's very practical and shows they know what to do.'

Jen saw that the roses had wilted somewhat in the vase, having greedily drunk the water. She took hold of the bottle of rose wine and unscrewed the top.

'Mum uses lemonade to give them a pick me up, but this should be as good.'

She poured some into the vase then replaced the lid, placing the bottle back on the table next to the roses. Glad of the few moment's distraction, she then moved to the next room, her bedroom at the front of the building, aware that her escort was following on.

The same scene applied here. Every drawer had been emptied and the contents discarded like rags or so much bric-a-brac, including her best silk lingerie — she so wanted to collect them up and put them out of sight — practical and sporty options were there as well for her more practical and active pursuits.

Trinket boxes lay empty on the bed as did her handbags, which had been stored in the overhead unit.

'Please don't touch anything or tidy up until the CSI guy arrives.' Lee started taking some notes.

Jen sighed. 'I don't think I can sleep in here tonight,' she said, swallowing hard. She looked out of her window across to the park the other side of the road and watched people walking by carrying on their normal lives as she would have been doing; relaxing into her weekend. Only now hers seemed very strange, as if she had been made to stop time itself as she was unable to touch any of her own things.

She had hoped for a well earned break and to enjoy a self-indulgent weekend as she had intended to, one in which she could take stock of her life, the material accumulation of which was displayed before her. Now Jen was being forced into taking account of it in a very different way.

'It might help if you also made a note of anything that is notably missing. If you could describe jewellery and valuables. If there's anything unusual missing, then it would give us a clear piece of evidence that can be linked directly back to you, if we discover them, that is. Also if there are any marks, scratches or damaged pieces, something that would make them unique.'

'I'll do that. I'll just get the notepad I use for shopping lists from the kitchen.'

She turned to leave the room, but stared out of the window as movements across the road in the park caught her eye. Fancy seeing Michelle there, she thought and decided that she would definitely speak to the girl and her grandmother on Monday. The child, somehow, knew something which would help her to clear up what had been happening in her life. Of this Jen was sure, yet she could not say why. It was just a feeling she had.

'You planning to go on holiday?' Sergeant Lee's voice asked.

His question surprised her. It seemed like he was now psychic and it was out of context with the current situation.

Jen had been watching a group of youths playing with a football on the grass opposite. Would it be too clichéd for it to have been one of them, she wondered. They had hoods, but having seen the force that must have been needed to split her door's panel apart from its frame, she reasoned this was not the answer. It would be too obvious, convenient and straightforward. Nothing in her life at that moment seemed to be the latter.

Jen glanced back and saw Sergeant Lee bending over looking at her guidebook of *Places to see in Hong Kong*, but without touching it.

Jen had to laugh at herself. Her paranoia was now imagining people to be psychic — how neurotic was that?

'Yes,' she said. The definite way she answered him even surprised her. The idea had been in her mind for long enough and she had been playing with the notion of venturing far beyond her comfort zone for a while.

Today she was certain that now that time had come. This apartment no longer represented a comfort zone, not as it was. It may well again, but for the present it seemed to have turned against her and she was not sure how long the change back to peace would take.

'You should go there. It's a fascinating place, changed phenomenally from the way it had been left before the handover. Now it's very modern and quite easy to get around.'

Lee looked at her, enthusiasm showing in his eyes, revealing a more youthful energy than his previous dutiful manner had. Jen stared at him. Again he seemed a little uneasy that he had perhaps said too much, showing another side of his personality than that of law enforcement officer. However, there had been such enthusiasm in his words when he spoke of the place that it was as if he had a genuine love of it as well as knowledge of its recent history, it seemed.

It was a contagious enthusiasm and despite the chaos and destruction that surrounded her she caught hold of his words feeling swept away with a desire to book up for her dream holiday, there and then.

'You sound as if you know it very well.'

'I do, my father's family came from there,' he said casually.

'Did they live there as expats when it was still a colony?' she asked, genuinely interested, but then as he half grinned at her, she realised that he meant his mother was from the country, as in being a native of the place, as Jen was to England.

She looked at his eyes afresh and his clearly defined features. Of course, that was why she had known that his golden brown skin colouring wasn't something he had acquired from any English summer. Yes, she could see now, although his facial features were more western in shape, which was why she had thought his strong features and good looks were simply down to the darkness of his eyes and hair . . . and his name, of course — Sergeant Lee.

'No, my father was actually from Hong Kong, so I'm half Chinese,' he said and returned to business. 'That's the cigarette wrapper there. Please don't touch it.'

Seemingly ignoring his comment, her head shot around in the direction of the dining-room. 'My passport!'

She ran into the living room and stared at the upside down drawer from her desk. She got a pencil and carefully slipped it under the edge of the wood, raising it up as she peeked underneath. There was an unopened tapestry wallet, which she flicked out from its hiding place with the pencil, letting the drawer fall freely back, untouched, upon the rug on her floor. She quickly opened the wallet; it acted as a cover for her passport and also included her NI card and driving licence.

Jen realised that a car was an expense she didn't need, but she had parted with some of the money her grandfather had left her as an inheritance on her car, rather than committing it to helping Harris to extend his house to include a room for a gym at the back of it. He said it would be an investment as he could do personal training in it. Her decision not to do as he wished had caused their first major rift as his insistence had become almost a demand, a test of her love and commitment to him. She saw it as nothing short of emotional blackmail.

He had furthered this by trying to undermine her confidence by correcting her every move behind the wheel of his car when she drove it, insisting that he parked the car unless it was in an open car park, like the one at the shopping mall. Like the house, she was reminded that the car was his. Like the children in the classroom, she had reminded him of the importance of sharing, especially as he was after her money to extend 'his' home, which in every way except for on legal documents was supposed to be 'theirs'.

'Ah, I can see you've watched CSI on the TV.' Lee risked a cheeky grin at her expense.

Jen stood up and placed the pencil

back in the pot, feeling quite pleased with her careful retrieval as well as relieved that her ID at least, seemed to be intact.

'My passport's there, but I think he's taken some jewellery, watches and some of my cash. I had two twenty pound notes on the top of the desk ready for tonight.' She sighed heavily.

'If we could have a list, it would help. The sooner we can track any individual items to the 'cash for gold' shops, then the sooner we may be able to pick them up. Also, if you could be specific about any item which could uniquely tie it in to this robbery, like an engraving on a watch, anything really, it would help tremendously.'

Jen retrieved a pen and tore a piece of paper from her notepad and started to make a cursory list of the small items which had been taken. Mainly her limited jewellery and watch, a camera and . . . she couldn't be certain, but her old diary and a spare key had gone from the hook. Unless it was on the floor under all the mess or Mr Marshall had it. Either way, whether the fingerprint man came or not, Jen had decided she was not staying the night there.

'This is all I can be sure has gone for now until I can touch things again and sort out this mess. I've written my mobile number on there. I'll not be here tonight.'

Jen gave him the list, determined that she would not stay in the flat until it could be made to look like her home again and the door had been made safe.

'Remember, Jen, you need to secure the back door once our man has been. I'll see you later because I need to sort some things out. If I'm very late then I'll pop down in the morning or if we turn anything up in the meantime.' He clipped her note in his file pocket. 'I'll give you my direct number and you can call me any time. Could you let me know where you are if you decide not to stay here?'

'Very well. I'll text or call in the details.'

She looked at him, expecting him to give her his card or something, and go, but he didn't. Instead he looked at her.

'Earlier you asked if something else had happened,' he said. 'Were you just referring to the flat tyre and the tack? Or was there anything else?'

Jen hesitated a moment. Now could be her time to disclose the truth of what had been happening throughout the week — but how to begin? She could start by mentioning the innocuous petals left as a gift, or the more menacing maggots appearing in the chocolate box. Perhaps she could ask him to trace the calls.

'Well, I've had a strange week. It started on Monday when — '

'Jen!' the unmistakably familiar voice of Harris resounded from the kitchen.

Jen looked at Sergeant Lee and mouthed one word, in yet more disbelief.

'Harris?'

Her fists instantly clenched at her side. If this was Sheila's doing, then school was going to be a very turbulent place on Monday morning. How else did he know what was happening, unless he had been stalking her.

Ever demanding, came the second call, 'Jen!'

8

Jen stared at Sergeant Lee who was watching her with a questioning look on his face.

'My ex,' she explained. 'My *very* ex,' she added, wondering why she had been so honest, again. The answer was that Jen wanted him to know. Too many unexplained events haunted her like the dream. Now, he was here, in her apartment and with all her heart she had no wish to be alone with Harris. Sergeant Lee picked up her unspoken plea.

'Please don't touch anything, sir,' Lee said firmly. 'This is a crime scene.'

Harris was just entering the kitchen, pushing aside the broken door and stopped momentarily and looked around at the clutter on the floor as he strode to meet Jen who had moved into the dining-room. He acted as if

189

he had not even heard Sergeant Lee.

'Bloody hell, Jen!'

He gestured at the mess all around him with his hands outstretched, emphasising the movement, giving a more dramatic effect; the same muscular arms that not so long ago Jen had happily run into.

Inwardly she cringed; what a fool she had been.

'What happened here? I know you're not keen on housework, but this is a bit extreme!' He half smiled, then returned to the gravity of the situation as if he realised his words were out of place in this situation. His face changed to a more sombre expression. 'Are you OK? Tell me what the hell happened here and I'll see if I can sort it out for you.'

Jen was transfixed as she stared back at him. The man's attitude was incredulous. He was a head taller than her, sturdily built and looked a solid reliable sort, or at least she had thought he was through her rose-tinted specs — now shattered. She had lost them thanks to Harris's constant demands upon her and also with the help of a clichéd buxom blonde called Kylie, three days into the New Year.

Jen was so surprised to see Harris there, in her new space, that she had almost forgotten about Sergeant Lee, who she caught sight of still standing in the doorway of her bedroom, observing this reunion and taking in every detail of it.

'Burglary . . . ' she blurted out, forcing herself to say something, while almost choking on the many things she would like to voice openly, to clear the air as Sheila kept reminding her she should do — but not in front of the law.

Harris boldly stepped in front of her, wrapped his arms around her waist and rested his head on hers as he pulled her in close to him.

Jen neither melted into his arms nor pulled away; she remained like a plank, unyielding and strong. She was stunned by his presence and by the fact that she felt absolutely nothing at his touch, when only a year ago she had been so in love with him that even just being next to him had made her feel warm and excited and had set her heart aflame with a longing to help this discarded soldier and help him find his way again.

'Are you hurt?' he asked, pulling away from her as he had obviously sensed her lack of response and had, it appeared, been taken aback by it. Placing a strong hand on each of her shoulders he stared directly into her eyes. 'Were you here when he broke in? Did you see him?' he fired a string of seemingly concerned questions at her. 'Did he do anything at all to you, Jen? What did the sod look like ... ? I'll ... '

'No, I was at work,' she answered, beginning to wonder how he knew where she had moved to. She had definitely not given a forwarding address when she left his house. 'How did you know where I was, Harris?' she asked, the stunned feeling which surrounded her starting to lift. A cold anger was rising to fill the space it had left behind.

'Well, I have ways. You know I want to make sure you're safe, Jen. Just because we had a tiff doesn't mean I don't love you, does it?' When she did not respond he continued, 'I came around to talk to you, or at least to leave a note for you to pick up when you got back from work, and look what I find. A right mess and you lost in the middle of it!'

He stared at her and ploughed on with, 'Look, this is precisely why we should never have split up, Jen. You need someone to look after you. You tried the independent woman thing and we can see where it's landed you. Come back to my place — to ours — and let's just talk. You can't stay here, that's obvious. It just isn't safe anymore, is it? Just for tonight and then tomorrow I'll help you check this lot. I'll skip gym tonight. Kev will understand, and I'll sort out what you need to do. You'll need to claim insurance and . . . ' His head spun around to look at the figure emerging from her bedroom doorway. 'Who the bloody hell are you?'

He turned his surprised expression to meet Jen's annoyed one as she stared back at him as defiantly as she could.

'I'm Sergeant Lee, and you are?' His voice was calm and perfectly even.

'Aren't you supposed to have the words 'police' written on your jacket?'

'Not always, the patterned car parked outside usually helps. And you are . . . ?'

Jen noted how the mature officer attitude had re-emerged from the less formal manner he had slipped into when talking with her. The air almost prickled with tension from Harris, yet Sergeant Lee seemed completely indifferent to it.

Jen saw his observant eyes summing up Harris. He was at least a foot taller than her ex and dark in colouring, as Harris's hair was a cropped army style and sandy brown. Harris had been a sergeant also, but in the armed forces until two years ago when he came out after his several years' service. Both these men were trained to perform their duty, both were neat, both fit and both, Jen realised, were sizing the other one up.

If the situation was not so serious, and her despair not as amplified, she would have found the whole scenario quite funny; like two peacocks or bulldogs squaring up to the other in a silent moment of appraisal and challenge. Her money would have been on Lee. He was the calmer one, but a man she sensed had great inner strength.

'Have you caught him yet?' Harris asked bluntly.

Jen knew he could be that way. It was just his manner, she had excused it because of his hard man past but now saw it as part of the make-up of the bully who rants when he doesn't get his own way. She must really mean something to him, she realised, because he was trying to stay calm with her and not shout that she was a bloody fool, a stupid bitch, and that this was all her own fault for moving out in the first place.

Oh yes, Jen could picture the words flowing from his mouth just as she had dreamed about the flow of petals that had melted into blood — was it a prophecy? Was his tirade to come?

Jen noticed an instant glimmer of humour or sarcasm in the Sergeant's expression, which may have been too subtle for Harris to pick up on — or at least she hoped he hadn't because she didn't want him to over-react here and get arrested. She just wanted him out of her life.

'We're just assessing the scene, but I'm confident we shall.' Lee smiled politely, but Harris walked straight past him and entered Jen's bedroom.

She pursed her lips and was about to say something, but noticed that Sergeant Lee was following Harris inside, keeping him in view all the time.

'Please don't touch anything,' he said, but stopped as Harris had already bent over and picked up the cigarette packet from the floor. He looked at it and crumpled it into a ball in apparent disgust. 'Do not touch anything,' Lee repeated firmly.

'Jen!' Harris held the wrapper in his hand and showed it to her as she entered the room. 'Since when did you start smoking?' he asked.

'Sir, I must insist that you do not touch or disturb anything This is a crime scene.' Sergeant Lee spoke, but Harris's eyes did not move their attention from Jen's.

'Well?' he demanded. 'You know how I feel about smoking.'

'I haven't,' Jen answered, her eyes glancing at the face of the sergeant. Surely Harris was not going to have one of his displays of temper in front of the policeman?

She was amazed that she still had some vestige of care towards the man. He was a big enough boy to look out for himself, he did not need mothering.

'Then why is there an empty packet on your bedroom floor?'

Jen was so tempted to leave him wondering if someone else had been there with her. Then she saw Harris's eyes look upon her underwear as it lay exposed and she cringed. They were new, delicate and feminine. He had never bought her anything so tasteful and she had always worn sports bras and pants before.

'That's evidence,' Sergeant Lee snapped, 'Do not touch anything else. Crime Scene will be here shortly. They'll now need to take your fingerprints too,' Sergeant Lee added the last comment as he kept his attention firmly on Harris's reaction.

Jen's heart sank. She didn't want Harris to stay a second longer than he had to and she certainly did not want him given a legitimate excuse to be there. Jen was also amazed that a feeling of panic was starting to threaten her already tightened nerves. She did not want to be left in this mess with Harris on her own. She looked to Sergeant Lee, but she could hardly ask him to stay with her and babysit.

Harris tossed the wrapper onto the bed, hunching his shoulders as a child who was defensively shrugging off his wrong-doing or stupidity, yet not apologising for it.

'Look, I'll go. I'm obviously in the way of things here. Call me when you're done and I'll pick you up later, Jen.' Harris took a step forward to leave. 'You can give the policeman your number and I'll see you're safe.'

'It might be a good idea if you stayed and then they could take your prints too. It will make it easier to dismiss them from the investigation.' Lee stared at Harris in silent challenge.

Jen sensed an atmosphere of what she presumed was dislike or distrust in the man's voice.

'That won't be necessary seeing as I've not been in here before.' His remark was said dismissively. 'If you're not coming back to mine now, then I'll get to the gym and tell Kev I'll be leaving early.' He turned to face Jen. 'Call me, love and I'll pick you up later. We'll talk then.' He gave her a light peck on the cheek and patted her shoulder.

'No, Harris, I'll be fine.' her voice almost broke as she tried to control the words she spoke.

'Think on it,' he replied as he walked away. 'Call me,' he shouted back as he let himself out by the front door.

Jen stood there rather awkwardly. She so wanted to answer Harris in the manner her mind had formed words to do so, but with Sergeant Lee standing there listening, she did not want him to think that she was no more than a screaming Banshee.

The sergeant stood forward. 'This is my number, Miss Brightman. If you need help, or remember anything important that's missing then please phone me. I'm on late shift tonight and for the next four days. If we have any information we'll keep you informed.'

He gave her a card showing his name as Sergeant Aidan Lee.

She nodded and he stepped in front of her.

'Are you sure you're OK? That man Harris, is he a problem?'

She sensed he was letting the question drift off so that he did not have to finish it, but had thought that bluntness may be needed. He wanted her to explain their relationship for him.

'My ex, is the simplest way of describing Harris.'

She shrugged, embarrassed and still surprised that he had turned up at a time when she needed someone to be there for her. For once in their stormy relationship, she realised he had been there when help could have been needed, when she felt lonely and vulnerable. Then he had told her what to do without hearing any answer in reply. He was merely using a situation to try and get his own way again. As he always had. He clearly believed she would run back to him as if he was a shell she could hide within.

'What's his full name, miss?' Lee asked, his pen and notebook in hand, poised ready to write it down the detail.

'Harris G Dalton,' she answered. 'He works at the Stardust Gym in town. He manages it with another ex-army friend, Timothy Starr. He provided the initial set up cost — well most of it — and Harris is the man with the knowledge of how to run a gym and turn in a profit. He may lack subtlety, his past army life has left him like that, but he works hard.'

Jen cringed inwardly. What had possessed her to add the last comment she had no idea, other than she had almost felt ashamed at having admitted she had once been his girlfriend, even stating the 'ex' had linked her to him in a way that had made her feel ashamed — a double failure. Firstly, admitting that she had become involved with someone who had no respect for an independent woman, and secondly that the relationship had failed, albeit understandably.

'He's definitely not been in here before, miss?' he asked Jen thoughtfully.

'No, of that I'm sure. May I call you

Aidan? I am beginning to feel as though I'm back in the classroom with the 'Miss' tag and it seems strange calling you Sergeant.'

'Very well, Jen. Look, I shouldn't really offer this, but as we're neighbours, if you don't mind I'll borrow William's hammer and some nails and when I come back later I'll secure the door for you. Unless you want to ask someone else to do it — your ex perhaps?' It seemed his awkwardness had returned along with a need to discover truths.

'Harris is not going to be invited or encouraged to do anything, Aidan,' Jen said definitely. 'I would be carried off to his home and returning would be more awkward than it was when I left there initially. No, I won't be asking him for anything. Our short-lived romance died.'

'Mr Dalton is perhaps not sure you know your own mind?' he offered, but Jen sensed he was fishing for her reaction.

'Oh, he knows that I do, but he just wants to override it with whatever his is wanting.'

'Is he abusive?' he asked suddenly.

Jen ignored his remark; it was too complex for her to explain there and then. She felt overwhelmed by emotion and desperately tired. Exhausted by everything that had befallen her perfect world. Harris had capped it by his humiliating presence.

'If you would pop back, that would be very good of you. It would put my mind at rest.'

She swallowed. Her eyes were becoming moist and she was fighting the urge to sob. Self pity was not something she admired, especially within herself.

Aidan smiled. 'You need the place to be safe again.' He walked toward the back door. 'Phone anytime, if you need to,' he added as he stepped outside. 'If you know I'm in and need anything . . . if you need to talk to me about this — or him — then, please just come and get me.'

Jen watched him from her window as he sat in the car and talked into his radio before driving off. Now, she had to think quickly. Grabbing her handbag she pulled out her mobile. No new messages. There was a small B&B the other side of the park, which she had used when her relatives stayed on a visit.

Without hesitation she booked herself into a single room and left what had been her lovely new private space behind her, to come back if necessary for the prints and then leave it to face a fresh day with renewed energy and also to try and shake off the presence of Harris again.

★   ★   ★

Within half an hour she had another place to sleep where there was no clutter and a clean bed. She phoned Aidan Lee straight away, as she'd not waited for the CSI team to turn up.

He picked up the call almost instantly.

'Miss Brightman . . . Jen?' his voice showed that he was surprised to hear from her so soon after they'd parted. 'Is something wrong?'

'Hi, Sergeant . . . '

'Aidan,' he interrupted.

'I'm not at home at the moment. Can you ask your CSI people to phone this number when they're going to my flat and I'll meet them there?' She paused.

'Yes, of course, I will. Where are you? Are you OK?'

Jen was reluctant to tell anyone anything about her whereabouts. The certainty that she was in some way being targeted had not left her all week. However, Aidan Lee was supposed to be one of the good guys, so if she couldn't trust him, who could she?

'The Sea View B&B. Do you know it?' she asked.

'Well, I know of it. Not far away then. What room are you in?'

She swallowed, not knowing why, but

wishing anonymity was hers again. 'No, it's not far so I can be back in ten minutes. I'm in room eight.'

'Remember what I said, call any time.'

'Thank you. I'm fine, really.'

Jen hung up, relieved that she did not need to stay in her dream flat a moment longer, which had been so badly violated, firstly, by the burglar and then by Harris. He had walked into her bedroom as if he had every right to be there. The question as to the owner of the cigarette packet had shown a glint of the jealous lover, which she had seen before when he wrongly accused her of flirting.

Strange, though, as she studied the faded fringe on the pink bedside lamp, that she did not feel the same way about the presence of Sergeant Aidan Lee in her space, or of his questions. He had a gentle yet strong presence which had been very calming. One thing was for certain, he clearly had an instant dislike for Harris. His judgment of people was obviously greater and more perceptive than hers.

* * *

Aidan Lee sat a few moments in his car and called through straight away to the control room.

'I need a check done on a Harris G Dalton, ex-army, runs a gym in Ebton called Stardust Gym.'

Sergeant Lee waited while the name was checked on their system. He thought he had a good natural instinct for trouble. What a lovely looking young woman like Jennifer Brightman was doing mixed up with someone like Dalton he had no idea, but it appeared that she had seen the light. Or having ventured into the dark had fought her way out before the door was closed to her forever. It looked to him as though she'd had a narrow brush with a low-life.

'Yes, Lee here.' He listened intently. 'Thanks,' he replied, before driving off.

He prided himself on his natural instinct and it had been proven to be right again. Naïve Miss Brightman; he realised that she was not even aware of who it was she had tried to help.

★ ★ ★

Harris was livid. A bloody burglary! Yes, it could lever her back, but he had been in such a rush to get in there and talk to her that he had not even given the cop car a second glance. Was he losing his wits? He hadn't realised that the police car was there for her.

He left his car out front and stormed into the gym. It was quite a small space where a dozen people could work out comfortably in the basement of an old seaside hotel. In grander days it had been a private residence. Now it was a conglomeration of a gym on the basement floor, a café on the ground floor and a hair salon on the second. Each business complemented each other, but none was linked to the other.

'Hi, H. I didn't expect you to be here,' Kevin said, as he replaced a set of weights on the stand. 'When Sheila told me what had happened I couldn't believe your luck, mate. Jen'll be scared witless. As it was Sheila was practically shaking at the news. She said a cop had come into the classroom. I knew something had happened the minute I clapped eyes on her. She can't keep anything from me. Was the flat totally trashed then?'

'Messy, that's all. Typical grab and run job.'

Harris stomped over to Kevin, where there was a punch bag hanging in the corner beyond the weights section. Harris balled his fist and smashed it into the bag, which rebounded with the force of the blow.

'She hasn't agreed to come back to you then?' Kevin asked. 'Was she upset? She wouldn't let Sheila go down there, either. Don't know what's got into her with all this independence stuff. You two were great together.'

Harris turned and scowled at his friend.

'Not outright, she hasn't, but she will. I love her, you're right, we're meant to be. Never thought I would feel that way about a bit of class, Kev. She's good for me. When I'm living with her, I can behave like a real gent. Don't need my fix, just get on with stuff, but since she left, things have got bad again. I need her or I need the stuff.'

Harris slammed a punch into the bag again.

'Perhaps you should tell her. She might be able to help straighten you out. You know, touch her sense of duty . . . '

Harris rounded on him instantly.

'Duty? Duty! I fought for duty and where did it get me? Thrown out on the streets like a tramp, with no home, no job and no purpose. Even as a bouncer I ended up getting arrested! Give me an enemy to smash and I'll stalk 'em and obliterate the buggers. I don't like the world outside here, without the unit. I don't want people to feel pity for me.'

'Except Jen,' Kevin said and ducked as Harris's fist swung.

'Well, she did, H. Hitting me isn't going to change that.'

Harris punched the bag again in frustration.

'Well, she may have but only because we was meant to be together. Hell knows that I thought my heart was beyond being touched by sentiment, but Jenny did that. She got right under my shell and melted what I thought was set in stone. She ain't that special looking, even . . . well she is pretty with that fiery hair and those blue eyes, but she ain't no leggy blonde, like Kylie was. Still, she's for keeps. You don't let a girl like her go. She looked at me with that way of hers, as if she believed in me, hung on my every word. I never knew anyone who believed in me like that and I want her to look that way again. She doesn't hold her hand out for money or favours, she needs to learn to let a man look after her. I hadn't even told her that many lies. Why did she have to walk out when it all was going so well? I only wanted to make a home for her.'

'H, she's used to making her own decisions. That's why she's a teacher. She leads the kids,' Kevin offered.

'That's a woman over kids, but she needs me to look after her. It was that bloody inheritance that was the curse, set us apart. It gave her the opportunity to go and set up on her own. Before that I'd even talked to her about giving up her job. I mean, why would a woman want to fuss over everybody else's kids when she could look after her own? That would have grounded her. I can't understand it, one little slip with that Kylie bird and she walked. I was only testing the stuff.' He sighed.

'Perhaps you best take care if the police are sorting out this break in, H.' Kevin looked at his friend.

'If only she'd given the money up, spent it on doing up the place then we could have still been together. I need her to need me!' He stared at Kevin.

'Sheila says she'll come round soon. She's had a tough week. Once the fear of what's happened to her precious flat hits her, she'll come back, you'll see.' Kevin slapped his friend's broad shoulders. 'Come on, do a proper workout and it'll make you feel better.'

'You've been dead lucky with that wife of yours, Kev. She has her heart and her sense in the right place. Did you give her the earrings then?' Harris was grinning.

Kevin laughed. 'Yeh, thanks for that, I owe you. Never thought the nosey cow would have looked in the drawer.' Kevin looked at Harris. 'How much do I owe you for them?'

'On the house, mate. I sort of came by them anyway.' He winked and Kevin laughed at him.

'No expense spared!' Kevin quipped.

'Well, the bloody roses cost me a fortune.'

'Never mind, I did well out of it. Sheila won some money on the Bingo last Friday, so I got more than I bargained for. So tell me, did Jen say you could pick her up later then?'

Harris shrugged. 'Didn't have time to work on her properly. I'll go back later, though, 'cos I told her I would. She'll be there, and she'll agree then.'

'Why didn't you stay with her? I said I'd hold the fort here.'

'Thing is, we weren't alone. Bloody copper was there and he told us I have to have my prints taken too, so as to dismiss me from their enquiries.'

Kevin let out a low noise as he exhaled. 'Oh, hell, Harris!'

'Yep, that's what I thought. I saw the car outside, but thought it was to do with something going on in the park since there was one across the road too. He should have left when I arrived, but instead, he wanted to get me involved. Bad move, eh? Near miss, that one. It was a long time back, but I guess they don't delete records.'

Harris hit the bag again.

'So what now?' Kevin asked.

'I wait. I visit there one more time tonight, much later on, and then I give her another chance or offer to stay — sleep on the sofa to protect her and look pathetic and hangdog at her, show her how genuine I am if the roses didn't do the job already. It worked on her before, it will again, cos this time I mean it.'

'What about the fingerprints?' Kevin asked persistently.

'Didn't touch anything other than a ciggy wrapper and I made a right mess of that. Found it in her bedroom and thought, well . . . didn't think it through really. I picked it up without stopping to think. She wouldn't, not my Jen. Don't worry they won't be traceable, I don't think, not like that. Whoever broke in actually did me a big favour, it'll prove to the stupid woman at last that being on her own is a fool's game, but if I get my hands on them, I'll smash their face in.'

Kevin nodded agreement, but said nothing.

'Don't think that would be a good

idea. Look, if you're going to be here for a while I need to see to some things and then I'll pop back at our normal time. I've only seen the usuals so far, but the evening is young.'

Kevin paused and thought for a moment.

'Look, why don't you keep a low profile for a couple of days. Let my lass work on her on Monday and put a good word in for you. She says she's been doing her best all week. Then the cops will be out of there. They'll be lucky to catch the sod anyway, but you might with your contacts. Jen's not weak, Harris. She has the bit between her teeth at the moment and if she knew you're a user, she'd go so far away from you that not even a space shuttle could cover the distance.'

Harris thought deeply for a moment.

'I told her I'd pop back tonight. I'll see if she is ready to come then. If not, then I'll wait for the plodders to disperse before I try again. But, Kevin, she's mine. She just don't know how much she is yet. But she will.

9

Jen had placed her phone on silent. Habit, she guessed, or the desire not to be disturbed while she took an hour's kip. She was exhausted by the week and had needed to recharge her flagging energy levels and disperse the onset of a headache. It was all happening too fast.

Harris arriving had been the last straw and she'd found that his appearance in her flat was even more upsetting than the burglary. So he had her watched or knew where she was based.

Her phone rang at 9.35p.m. It was dark outside and Jen realised she had no desire to go out, but she took the call.

'Sergeant Lee.'

Relief flooded through her when he told her that CSI had another more urgent job to go to and would be there the next morning. That meant she didn't have to go back to the flat before daylight broke again, which meant there was no way that Harris would be able to try and collect her from there. She could face him in her own time when she was in control of her emotions and the mess had cleared. However, today was not going to be a day for a final showdown, not when she was so fraught.

Jen still needed to sort out a new back door and the insurance cover for it as soon as possible. She'd placed a call to them as soon as she had arrived at the hotel. Just to set things in motion.

'Thank you for ringing,' she told Aidan. 'Yes, I'm fine and thank you for making the flat secure. See you in the morning then. Night.' She rang off as soon as she could.

Jen was about to switch her phone off in order to have some peace during the night, when she remembered that she had forgotten to dial Sheila. She sighed, thought about not bothering, but then realised that was unfair.

Letting the phone ring, she watched the world go by from behind the net curtain at the window, though she didn't want to touch it as it looked like it could do with a good wash. Her own blinds were clean, fresh and . . . She missed her flat.

Not a lot was moving outside in the street, but the odd person wandered down to the pub on the corner. Both the hotel and the pub were nestled behind the park opposite her own apartment.

'Hello . . . Jen?' Sheila's anxious voice answered the call.

'Yes, it's me,' Jen admitted, feeling a little bit guilty.

'Where the hell are you? I tried calling the flat and your mobile but you've had it switched off for hours. I've been worried sick about you!' Sheila blustered.

'I had to crash out, you know, have a nap.' Jen felt it was a lame excuse.

'Well, tell me what's being going on and where you are.'

'It's messy, a few personal things were taken, jewellery, money, easily disposable stuff. The flat doesn't seem to have been damaged much at all, though.'

She watched the street lamp outside and looked at the shadows it cast on the wet pavement. The weather was dampening and casting a mist over the view.

'So where are you, Jen?' Sheila asked.

'Just somewhere I can find some peace and make sense of what's been happening to me of late,' Jen said vaguely. 'Mr Finch knows about the burglary and said that if I let him know on Sunday if I need time out on Monday that would be OK.'

'Well he should. Where's that you're staying? I told you that you could come here, didn't I?' Sheila sounded a little hurt.

'I asked you not to tell Harris about the burglary, but you must have. How else could he have known about it and where my new apartment was?'

Jen's voice was very calm as she

spoke, which surprised her, because after feeling so revolted, then angry, she had woken with a strange acceptance of what had happened. It was as if a voice inside her was telling her that this would bring everything to a head. She had thought of asking advice from the police about the texts and the gifts.

'No, I didn't! It wasn't like that,' Sheila protested. 'When Kevin saw me, he knew I was worried about something. I told him about the burglary and never said anything about involving Harris. I said you'd said it was OK and you'd phone later. How was I to know he would be straight on the phone to Harris,' Sheila tried to explain.

'I asked you not to involve them, Sheila,' Jen knew she sounded disappointed, but also felt justified.

'Kevin is my husband. I had to tell him. I could hardly hide it and couldn't make up a lie to cover why I was so concerned about you, that would have been worse. Besides, he's so worried about his friend — as I am mine. Why don't you go back with him until this is sorted out, Jen?'

Jen shook her head. 'You really don't understand. There is no going back.'

'Jen, all relationships hit awkward times. Harris is a good guy. He may be a little messed up by adjusting to life outside the forces, but you can sort him out. You already had, more than you realise. Just give him another chance. Tell him if you felt he was being a bit bossy. He'll understand.'

'I did. He threw it back in my face. He doesn't understand what being 'just' friends means. So there's no going back for us. I think he needs proper help, Sheila.' Jen waited while there was a slight pause

'But if you talked to him, you could be the person to lead him to it . . . Jen? You still there?'

Jen was watching a car, one she knew well, drive along the road. It had been going at speed until it came to the hotel. Instantly, realising her mistake that she had not gone far enough away she held her breath as she saw that it stopped suddenly as it passed her Mini. Damn! How tired was she that she had left such an obvious sign of her presence in full view of where he was likely to pass? Her pulse seemed to increase its beat as she watched the inevitable happen. If she could not face him in her own home, here in this B&B would be like being a cornered animal. She had to escape and quick.

'Got to go. Speak Monday. Bye!'

* * *

Harris pulled up outside the apartment block. Seeing that there were no cars parked up, he walked to where he heard a banging noise emanating from the side of the building. His frame filled the width of the alleyway as he saw a man hammering a piece of board into place over the hole in the door. He worked by the light of a security lamp.

'Where's Miss Brightman?' he asked. His shadow was cast over the crouched figure who had the hammer in his hand.

As the man's face turned to look back at him he realised that it was the blasted cop he'd met earlier. No uniform this time, just jeans and a sweatshirt. He hadn't walked far this night dressed like that. Harris was thinking that his presence at this hour, doing good deeds, was perhaps beyond the call of duty. He started to smell a rat — and he wondered if this rat had poisoned Jen's mind against him.

'Who wants to know?' Lee said, and continued hammering.

'I'm her boyfriend — her fiancé, actually.' Harris stood defiantly, resisting the urge to ball a fist and smash the supercilious guy's face into oblivion.

'That's not how you were described to me. She's not here.' Lee stood up having finished his job to his own satisfaction and still holding the hammer casually in his hand. He faced Harris.

'You threatening me, officer?' Harris

asked, sarcastically.

'I'm answering your question. This is private property and I advise you to leave it the same way you arrived — in haste. If Miss Brightman wants to speak with you she has your number.'

Harris's fist balled, unseen in the dark shadows his knuckles turned white, but he resisted the urge to strike out as he would end up in a cell and he'd been down that route before. No doubt this man knew that and was hoping he could get him sent down again. How convenient for him that would be if he was after his Jen. GBH second time around and against a copper; they'd throw away the key.

Instead, Harris took a step backwards. 'We'll see,' he barked out and reluctantly left.

Driving around the park, over the railway bridge, he thought about stopping at the pub on the corner and drowning his sorrows while he thought things through, but then a gift was given to him — a blessing from heaven.

Jen had wasted some of their gym money on a pretty new red Mini and there it was, parked outside The Seaview B&B. Harris smiled and pulled in. He knew the place well, had used it with some of his girls. Well, he'd had to try making a living somehow. Trouble was the wenches were too much hassle and he nearly had the place shut down when someone tipped off the cops what he was up to. Narrow escape that one.

Parking up, he sauntered inside. Good, Annie was sitting there manning the reception — well, she was sitting on her chair in the tiny room which had once been a downstairs dunny in the old house, before it was converted into a small B & B. With her cast off desk, originally from IKEA, this was now the reception and her office.

'Hi, sweet lady!' Harris said with a beaming smile, and leaned on the open doorway to her room. He saw her eyes roam over every detail of his muscular build, his T-shirt showing off the contours like a second skin.

'What you doing here, Dalton?' she asked.

'Come to see my good lady friend,' he said seductively, and continued to smile, his most beguiling one, as he leaned over to her, his mouth only millimetres from her ear. He saw her tense as she sat upright.

'I'm George's lady, not yours, H. You nearly got us closed down, you slime-bag.' Her words, softly spoken but almost hissed, tickled his ear.

He stroked her cheek with the back of one finger, gently running it along the line of her jaw, following the contour of her neck before tracing the line of her cleavage, noticing how her breasts rose in anticipation of his touch. He'd never lost it, but one woman wouldn't play with him, the only one he really wanted. With his breath warm on Annie's flesh, he whispered, 'Which room is Miss Jennifer Brightman in?'

'Now that would be telling and breaking guest confidentiality,' she whispered back.

'Then tell?' he answered, still toying with her, his finger slipping inside her blouse. He could almost feel her quiver.

'It'll cost you twenty,' she said, and slumped back in her chair grinning at him.

Still grinning, he pulled out his wallet, took out a twenty pound note, and held it in front of her. 'Which room, Annie?'

She held her hand out for it, but he shoved it into her cleavage. 'It'll be all warm and cosy,' he quipped.

She laughed, pulling it out and putting it in the pocket of her jeans. 'Number eight, but Harris, you create any trouble and I'll call the cops on you. I mean it.' Her manner was now dead serious. 'George nearly set the lads on you last time, so be a good boy, eh?'

Harris nodded. 'Always am, Annie, just misunderstood, that's all. You wouldn't have a spare key, would you? I'd like to surprise her,' he asked innocently.

'You couldn't afford that. Go on with you, or I'll have to phone George and disturb his game. Don't want that do you?'

'Nope.' He took the stairs two at a time. There was no way he wanted that.

★　★　★

Jen had placed the 'Do Not Disturb' sign on the door to buy her time. Possibly seconds, but it might work.

Seeing Harris park outside she knew her hideaway had been discovered by her own stupidity and lack of thought. This time it was not through her over zealous friend, but because she'd not had the sense she was born with and had parked her bright red new Mini outside the place she was staying only a stone's throw away from where her flat was. This town was too small.

Suddenly, she realised that instead of moving only a town away from Harris, she should have just moved region or country, but then that was like running away from problems and she always prided herself on facing up to them.

There was one central staircase up to the two halves of the house, a simple arrangement of two rooms either side on two floors. Her room was on the top left.

Jen stood in the shadows as Harris climbed the stairs silently, two at a time, on the old carpet and watched as he turned to the door of the room she had paid for. Were they supposed to give out the guests' room numbers to just anyone, she wondered even as she held her breath?

He took the 'Do Not Disturb' sign off and scrunched it up, tossing it into a flower pot on the window sill. She watched from the other side of the stairs, behind the door of a cupboard where the new linen and cleaning materials were stored and held her breath as long as she could, slowly letting it out as if he had extra-sensory powers and could home in on it.

Harris raised his fist and knocked

once on the door.

No reply.

He shifted his weight from one foot to the other. Knocked once more, with more force this time. His stance was agitated.

No reply.

She saw him standing there, fists formed, the image of a very angry man.

'Jen!' he snapped. 'Come on. It's me. We need to speak. What you doing in a dive like this when we could be at home together? Look we need to talk. Come on, open the door and stop playing games . . . '

She saw him curse and for a moment her world stopped as he looked across and then down the stairwell.

Jen breathed again as he returned his attention to the door. Harris fidgeted in his pocket and took something out of it which was too small to determine from where she was, but it soon became apparent what it was and she ducked back as he glanced around him again.

Then she watched this man she

thought she had once known well pick the lock to her hotel room. Her jaw dropped open, but she stifled the desire to gasp in horror that her ex went around with a pick-lock in his pocket.

The second he slipped inside the room she ran down the two flights of stairs, passing the stunned woman on the reception desk and climbed straight into her Mini. Throwing her bag on the passenger seat she drove. Leaving at speed, she did two blocks, then circled back, taking the first turning up an alleyway where she turned out the lights of her car and locked her doors.

Only a few moments later she heard Harris's car rev as he started his engine and sped off in the direction of her apartment.

She wasted no more time. Her hand was shaking but her mind was made up as she pulled out her mobile phone from her handbag and dialled.

★　★　★

Harris drove around by the apartment but Jen had not returned there.

'Damnation!' he shouted angrily and then made his way back to the gym. He was going to have to do the workout from hell or he would burst and smash someone's face in.

That woman was driving him to breaking point. He'd have to get a fix and find someone who he could release his feelings on. It was her fault, all of it. He had been a patient man, but she was pushing him too far.

Jen must have seen him come in and had hidden from him and then run. Why? She didn't know any of the bad stuff, yet she'd still turned on him.

'One more chance, Miss B, don't blow it.'

His words were only heard by him as he stormed back into the gym, entered the back office, removed the supply of membership cards from the drawer and took one of the small bags underneath.

'On the house, Harris. You earned it.'

10

The flat of number two was similar in layout to her own. The main difference, other than it was bigger, was that it had an extra bedroom.

Aidan had surprised her by revealing that he used Mr Marshall's garage next to their building to keep his motorbike in. With only this and a few neatly stored tools inside it, there was plenty of space for her Mini to be secreted away from prying eyes. Mr Marshall left his own car on the drive as it was too difficult for him to manoeuvre in and out of the garage. The two men were obviously well acquainted with each other, as this arrangement seemed to be quite casual.

Once seated on a soft sofa inside Aidan's living room, she took time to admire the way western modern had been decorated with individual pieces of the orient.

He wasted no time in asking her a direct question. 'So, do you want to make legal moves to have a restraining order put on this man?' Aidan's face was very serious.

'He's never hurt or even threatened me. He just can't accept that it's over and I won't go back to him or ask him for help. I don't think he would ever actually harm me — or at least I didn't think he would.'

She fiddled with her fingers on her lap, like a nervous child and had to look away as the meaning of what she had just said sank in to both of them.

At that moment the realisation that she did not know how much danger she was in hit her hard. It seemed so alien to her to think that the controlling relationship she had become entrapped within was now turning into a possible abusive or threatening situation, one which could escalate in a physical sense. Jen had never imagined her life could become so dark and complicated. This was the sort of thing that happened to other people in the news or on TV dramas, not in her life.

Her own arrogance at thinking in such a way, was yet another shock to her; why should she be any different?

'So what changed your mind tonight?' Aidan had openly welcomed her into his home, made her a drink and seated her down on his tapestry settee. He sat on a chair opposite, giving her some space.

'I was at the hotel, as I said. I was talking to Sheila on the phone and staring out at the street when his car stopped as he passed by my Mini. I knew he'd recognised it and I picked up my bag and hid in a store cupboard on the opposite landing ... that might sound stupid to you.'

She looked at him for what she hoped would be a sign of understanding or approval.

'Actually, you were very quick-witted. You did the right thing.' He nodded back to her. 'If he'd entered the room with you in it, you would have been trapped as I doubt he would have left without creating a scene . . . or possibly worse.'

Jen was definitely getting the impression that Aidan Lee did not like Harris or think very highly of him.

'Well, from there I watched him. I did think he might just leave when I didn't answer, but in case he didn't, I decided I would wait until he was engrossed on shouting through the door and then try and slip down the stairs unnoticed.'

She shook her head as if trying to fight off her own stupidity.

'However, what he did do shocked me. He picked the door lock and let himself inside, without waiting for me to answer. That was when I decided to run, as soon as he stepped inside the room. I didn't know that he could do things like that. How many people walk around with picklocks in their pocket?' Jen asked, and as she was staring at him realised that, as he was a policeman, he had no doubt met quite a few.

Jen was so worried by everything that had happened to her in such a short time. What she could not fully understand was why she was telling all this to a comparative stranger. He represented the law and she could get Harris into a lot of trouble, but she still didn't know if he really deserved such bother or if it had all become over-dramatised.

However, her suspicions were building that she really did not have any notion of who the real Harris G Dalton was, only the person he had revealed to her. Yet, as she looked at Aidan, she didn't see a man who represented an impersonal uniform looking back at her, but someone she felt she could trust. He was her neighbour and now was rapidly becoming a much needed friend.

'Did you know he's been arrested for violence in the past?' Aidan said, watching her carefully. Jen could not hide her shock as he went on, 'He has a criminal record, Jen. Sure, he served in the army, but he's had problems before and since, possibly during as well. He was put away — has done time — for assaulting a man in an attempted robbery at a night club. He's known to us, Jen — the police, that is.'

He waited in silence for her response.

'Oh, I see. I've been a complete fool, haven't I?' she said, fighting the urge to dissolve into tears and sink into the sofa in an effort to just disappear.

'No, not a fool; perhaps just a little bit gullible,' Aidan said gently. 'And you seem to have kept him very quiet while you were with him, as if he's been on his best behaviour. Prior to you, though, the town became a more interesting place when Harris G Dalton and a friend of his arrived. Although he's had few scrapes, he narrowly escaped being brought in last time.'

Aidan leaned forward. 'I'm sharing this information with you for your own good. You must take care if he's around you now. You can't rely on any previous good behaviour to be extended to you anymore. He could turn at any moment. You need to know the kind of person he really is.'

Jen simply sat as a strange numbness swept her body. She sipped her tea, grateful for its warmth and trying to trigger some sense of feeling again.

'I thought he was an ex-soldier who had made a new life by building up the gym from a rundown basement. I thought I'd helped him to feel he was worth something and could contribute to society instead of feeling discarded by it. I even helped his literacy skills; writing had never been his favourite pastime. I thought . . . '

She stopped talking as the sought after feelings threatened to overwhelm her in a wave of pent up emotion. How could she have been such a naïve fool?

'Oh, I think you did all of those things,' Aidan agreed. 'But, Jen, you're worth more than that. If he really wants help, he could get it. You left him because you needed more from life and the point is that I think he knows that too. That's why he wants you to go back to him, to be dependent upon him. Jen, I'm no psychologist, but I strongly suspect he would have drained your spirit and still ended up being a right b — ' Aidan stopped himself and paused before continuing. 'His record shows that he tries one thing, gets bored or fails, then tries another. Easy money, usually, quick fixes — not someone who really works at a problem and strives to make a good living out of their own efforts. He leapfrogs off the backs of others.'

Aidan sighed heavily. 'I'm sorry to be so blunt, Jen. Feel free to tell me to mind my own business and go back to just being the copper and seeing to your burglary and being a good neighbour at the weekend. But it won't change the truth.'

'Considering I'm in your flat, drinking your tea and asking for your help, it would be high-handed of me to say that. I can't stand being in a room alone with him now. I didn't know about his temper outbursts until we moved in together and I started to express my own will. I don't know what to do anymore, Aidan. My flat is spoilt, my peace shattered — and one of my closest friends thinks I should be back with him. Her husband, Kevin, is one of his best friends and — '

'Who is this?' Aidan interrupted.

'Kevin Simms, he's a PE teacher in St Peter's Senior School. They've known each other for years through the gym. Sheila, his wife — you saw her in the classroom — she works with me as my teaching assistant. She thinks I'm good for Harris and that he's a solid reliable chap! So the whole situation has become very complicated and claustrophobic. It's like my home life and work-place have meshed together and I'm caught in between the two. I feel totally trapped.'

Jen looked at him with moist eyes. 'You've been honest with me, Aidan, so answer me truthfully . . . do you think I'm a complete fool?'

'Not at all, but if I am honest, which

I normally am, I do think you've been used. So tell me about the 'something else' you mentioned before Dalton turned up. What happened on Monday that you tried to tell me about?'

He leaned forward, his hands interlocked as he rested his elbows upon his knees. He certainly wasn't giving the impression that he thought she was neurotic.

'Petals happened.'

He raised his eyebrows and Jen explained about finding the cascade of petals in her mail box. It wasn't long before he had taken out a notepad and jotted down names, events and times.

'So you don't think I'm making more of this than just a prank, then?' she asked. 'I mean they could be seen as simple gifts.' She desperately wanted to have his opinion on this.

'Not at all, Jen. You say you deleted the messages from your mobile unintentionally.'

'By accident, yes. I was thinking of doing it, then decided not to, but when

I was caught with my phone in my hand, by one of the students, I accidentally hit the 'yes' on the touch screen and they were gone.' She shrugged as if to say that she was a fool for doing it, but that it was too late, the damage had been done.

'Well they weren't actually malicious in content, so were not offences or threatening in themselves. However, you say you repeatedly dialled the number and the phone was always turned off, or at least unavailable?' He smiled at her.

'I don't see why that's humorous at all.'

Jen watched him hold out his hand.

'The number will be in your call log as a dialled number unless you deleted that too. If you let me have it, I can see if we can trace it, but I suspect it'll be a pay as you go sim card so it may be untraceable. They need to be registered, but it depends on how accurate the registration detail is.'

Jen flicked through the menus and

found the log where the number was still stored, then passed the phone to Aidan, who carefully made a note of it. He tried redialling it, but it was still unavailable and he gave her the phone back.

'Tomorrow, I'll talk to the unit when they arrive and make sure that the bottle of wine is dusted for prints and that we look at the cards.'

'Mr Marshall's prints will be on it,' Jen remembered. 'He found it outside the flats and came to the door to give it to me.'

'No problem,' Aidan said. 'I'll see if there is anything to be gleaned from the mailbox, too. One way or another we'll unearth this mystery person. Like you, I don't think this is the work of the likes of Harris, but there's something going on and you have every right to feel disturbed by it.'

'You don't think I am just being paranoid then?' Jen asked.

'No, Jen. I think you're being hounded and I don't see why you should be. It could even be that Dalton is one problem, the messages and gifts are another and the burglary is something separate again. There were two others down the road this evening, which points more towards someone on a run for quick cash. Could be for money, or goods which are easily converted into cash, to feed a drug habit. Possibly to buy their Meow.'

'Sorry? Their cat?' Jen was so tired for a moment she thought she had missed something.

'No, drugs — Meow Meow — M Cat.'

'Is that what they're known as?' She looked horrified.

'You've never heard of these kinds of recreational drugs?'

'Yes, of course. I've just not kept up with the names. I don't do them.' She blushed. 'I know that one is not illegal as I heard Harris talking to a friend who uses it, and he told me it wasn't, but I didn't want any.'

'Good.' Aidan stood up.

'Oh, I'm not sure what he was talking about, to be honest. I may have got the terms mixed up. I thought that was the name of something he was talking on the phone about one time, but so many of them have letters in their names, like the performance drinks and things that he uses at the gym.'

'If you remember any of the ones he specifically mentioned in his phonecalls or conversations then let me know, please.'

Jen also stood up and looked up into his eyes. He took a step towards her.

'I'm so tired,' she said.

Aidan put his arm around her shoulders in a naturally protective manner as he steered her toward the door off the short corridor. She let her head rest on him and was pleasantly surprised when she felt his hand run through her hair.

They stopped by the door and she faced him as his fingers let her hair fall back on her shoulder.

'Sorry,' he said, suddenly self-aware

and awkward. 'but it's such a beautiful colour.'

Jen smiled but it turned into a stifled yawn which she tried to cover with her hand.

'Sorry again — I really should let you get some sleep. You must be exhausted.'

He opened a door and showed her a small bedroom in which there was a single bed already freshly made up. The room was decorated in pastel shades giving it the feel of being much more spacious than it actually was.'

'This is so good of you.'

'It's no problem, Jen, really. Well, good night, sleep well.'

He walked back to the living room leaving her to settle.

Despite her initial awkwardness, her uneasiness soon passed as she fell into bed and slept solidly until a faint tapping on her door woke her.

Standing with her mass of tousled auburn hair, her strappy vest top and a simple pair of running shorts, Jen slowly opened the door and saw Aidan standing there dressed in jeans and a figure-hugging long sleeved black polo accentuating his strong features and muscular form. He was holding a mug of coffee.

'They'll be wanting to see you in your flat in half an hour,' he told her. 'Coffee's freshly brewed.'

He smiled at her as she saw him discreetly take in her attire and the contours of her body beneath it.

Shyly, Jen retreated behind the door and made straight for the bathroom. Twenty minutes later she emerged, quickly washed, groomed, simply made-up to accentuate her natural colouring and wearing jeans with a navy Henley shirt.

They sat down to a light breakfast together, with no air of awkwardness between them; both happy to sit and chat.

Hong Kong featured in their conversation, as he knew it well and she so wanted to go and explore the islands. When another twenty minutes passed by in a blink, she said she would get her bag, and head down stairs.

'Why not leave it there?' Aidan looked a little awkward, but then added. 'You may as well use the room for another night until you've sorted your place out. It's conveniently close by and I'll be on late shift, so I won't be around to disturb you.'

'You are very trusting for a police-man, aren't you?' Jen asked as she grabbed her keys.'

'Selectively so,' he said as he opened the flat door and led the way down the stairs to her flat. They had just entered her kitchen when the car drew up outside.

'Good, now to work.' He winked at her as he started looking around the place.

Jen had walked into the living area, really glad that her glass table had been left in one piece, but as she looked to the vase of roses on it she gasped.

'What's happened?' Lee asked. He was there in a flash.

'The roses — look, they're all dead!' she exclaimed as she pointed at them. Where a dozen new rosebuds had stood proud, instead of blooming in all their glory they had drooped and died; their beauty gone. The vibrant red disappeared, as if the life had been drained from them, leaving only wizened shells.

She looked at them feeling a tremble deep inside her soul. 'How? Aidan, they were so beautiful, and now . . . ' she gulped.

It was a slightly surprised crime scene investigator who entered the flat and found the owner of it sobbing her heart out on Sergeant Lee's designer top.

Jen pulled herself together when Aidan had, after a few moments of quietly hugging her, brought the tone of his professional voice back into the scene.

'Could you take James around and answer any questions regarding your possessions, Jen?'

She stepped back and nodded that

she was fine and took the man around her flat so that he could sort out what was a possible source of prints and what was not. Jen had to have hers taken so that they could be eliminated from the results.

'Make sure you take the bottle.'

Aidan pointed to the gift of wine, and then he looked at Jen.

'You topped the roses' water up with it, remember? I think it may well have something added to it. In which case, it's just as well you prefer Merlot.'

'How do you know that?' she asked, doubt creeping into her voice again.

He casually nodded towards her wine rack in the corner of the room, tucked at the side of her desk. It had half a dozen bottles laid in it.

Jen half smiled. She suddenly had the urge to leave them to it and, excusing herself she went to her bathroom, where nothing had been disturbed and just breathed deeply.

She pulled out her phone and looked at the call log. The number was there.

She followed her instinct and rang it, waited, listening to it ring. *Yes!* she thought, a result, and then nothing as it just rang out. *Damn!* She would try again later.

Jen freshened herself up and strode out to face more questions as now it seemed there was some proof that someone had wanted to hurt her. She felt an ice chill inside her, as she realised she had offered the bottle of wine to Mr Marshall. The question was, who was it and why?

11

Jen spent the rest of the day cleaning, sorting and reorganising her living space so that she could make yet another new start in her home.

She still loved her apartment. Knowing that the burglary had been a ten minute smash and grab somehow made it more bearable along with understanding that this at least had not been targeted specifically at her.

Once she was satisfied that the arrangement was sufficiently different from the original — although her options were somewhat restricted by the small space of her apartment's layout — Mr Marshall helped her to sort out the replacement door.

He went to the showroom with her and, with Aidan's suggestions in mind, they selected a suitable available design, fully glazed in a frosted pattern, which would fit in with the least fuss. The insurance company would cover this cost, at least that had been agreed.

Jen was so grateful that Mr Marshall also could oversee the men who came to fit it in, as she really wanted to get back to work — and normality — as soon as she could.

She was very relieved that there were no more messages for her left on her phone, so now she could honestly say that she almost felt safe. Harris had stayed away and she had felt as though she was free to live her own life again.

Aidan Lee had brought a feeling of stability back to her life.

She had also shared Friday and Saturday evenings in his apartment discussing Hong Kong and her summer plans. He was full of suggestions of places to visit and stay, locations that might interest her and things to try while she was there — as well as others to avoid.

Meanwhile, his concern for her seemed to have grown. He insisted that for her own safety she text him as to when she would return to the flat and also the minute anything unexpected happened or arrived.

Far from feeling controlled by this request in the way she did when Harris had tried to order her about, she found wisdom and genuine concern in his words.

* * *

Early Monday morning, Jen's mobile rang. It was a message from Aidan. He was reminding her to take care and also informing Jen that he would be in later than expected as a young woman had reported being attacked the previous evening. The circumstances were suspicious as the last thing she'd remembered was drinking with her friends after a night out; she had been found in a shelter on the seafront, completely disorientated and frightened, not knowing what had happened.

'Date-rape drugs, a coward's weapon

on the unsuspecting,' had been Aidan's comment.

Jen thought it was sweet that he had almost apologised for not being there as he'd promised he would be, and that he had thought to call her.

He assured her that he would text her when he returned, but she was to text him if she needed anything before then. He was certainly treating her situation as serious, and not being dismissive of her fears at all.

★　★　★

'Morning, Jen.' Sheila was already waiting for her in the classroom when she arrived at school. 'I was so worried about you. You cut our call so short that I didn't know what to think, and then I couldn't get an answer when I called back.' Sheila looked at Jen intently. 'Is everything sorted out now?' she asked, as they settled in for the day.

'Yes, all sorted. They've taken prints off anything and everything they could and arrested a guy who was caught for a couple of burglaries further down the road. He's been detained; he had items from those and another break-in from last week in his place. So it looks like I was just plain unfortunate as he was taking pot-luck chances and not singling out anyone in particular.'

Jen shrugged sadly and sighed. 'If only people would take less and share more.'

'A very noble sentiment, but we're talking about real life here not about children being nice to each other. I did say you were getting everything out of perspective. So, when are you seeing Harris again? Kevin told me he rushed around to help you out.' Shelia asked her, just before the bell went.

'I'll let them in,' Jen spoke quickly and walked off. It was going to be a long week if it started on a note like that. Somehow she had to break Sheila's persistent nagging that Harris was good for her and let her see what the man had been really like — but how?

When Jen opened the door she could see that a rather unhappy looking Michelle was being led inside by her grandmother. The woman was walking determinedly over to Jen, who quickly waved to Sheila, so that she could take over the door duty while Jen stepped inside to speak to Michelle and her grandmother in some privacy. She was sure the girl knew something, so perhaps she wouldn't have to wait very long to discover the truth.

'Miss Brightman?' the older woman asked politely.

Jen smiled at her warmly. 'Yes, I've been wanting to meet you.' Jen gestured that she should step further inside the classroom toward a quiet corner away from the coat racks.

'Good, because I want to speak to you too and dispel a malicious rumour which seems to be going around the classroom. It started, I believe, with a rather rude presumption by your helper.'

The woman looked pointedly at

Sheila, who was busy with the young children, although, Jen suspected, she was obviously trying to listen in on the conversation.

'I am sorry, but I don't quite understand what you're referring to.' Jen tried to keep her manner pleasant.

This was not the opening to the conversation she was hoping for. To be faced with a conflict situation, which this appeared to be developing into, so early on a morning and in the week, was not what Jen had expected.

'My daughter, Michelle, has been placed in a very difficult situation by your assistant who clearly does not know her facts. Michelle has informed me that you have all been referring to me as her grandmother since that woman called to Michelle across the classroom announcing that her gran had arrived to pick her up. Michelle was quite shocked as she'd not realised until that point that I was old enough to be her gran. She didn't know what to say and didn't want to look foolish in front of the other children or contradict her elders.'

The woman looked directly into Jen's eyes and added, 'I don't want to let this carry on, Miss Brightman. I'm her mother and I'll be at parents' night to see you about her work. I may be slightly more mature than your other mums, but personally, I don't see that as a negative thing.'

She looked directly at Sheila, her lips pursed.

Jen could clearly see that the woman was very proud of her role and also of her daughter, who had flushed red and was looking at Jen with a very guilty expression.

'I'm so sorry, this is most embarrassing, I should have checked the facts. I also presumed you must be a young grandmother rather than a more mature mother. I can only apologise for the unfortunate start. Michelle has been doing so well since she joined us in January. She's a lovely girl. Will you accept my sincere apology, and I'll make sure this is made known to everyone as discreetly as possible?'

Jen saw the woman continue to stare at Sheila.

'I also understand that Michelle was accused of being a liar by the same woman. I never want to hear such an accusation made again. My Michelle is not, and never has been, a liar.' The woman's cheeks were starting to redden slightly.

'I couldn't agree with you more.'

Jen's statement seemed to register deeply as Michelle's mother focussed on Jen's face instead.

'Michelle will be able to tell you that I've already sorted that misunderstanding out, haven't I, Michelle?' She looked at Michelle, whose cheeks were now a very rosy red.

'I told you that I loved my mummy too,' Michelle said.

'Yes, you did, and now I understand why you made that comment, although it would have been helpful if you could have pointed to your mummy at the same time,' Jen said kindly.

'Very well, then until parent's evening. I'll leave it at that, Miss Brightman.'

She bent over, gave Michelle a kiss on the cheek and left.

The children were now in and seated, and curious eyes had looked over to them, not least Sheila's.

Jen placed a hand on Michelle's shoulder, looked around the room and said loud enough for all to hear, 'Now that your mummy has gone, Michelle, go and hang up your coat.'

Sheila's eyes widened as did a number of the children's, but the misunderstanding had been dealt with.

Still, as Michelle walked away, Jen knew there were unfinished conversations to be had with her, but now she would have to be very careful how she worded her questions, as her mother was very intuitive and would no doubt be questioning Michelle about how things were going now.

'I thought she was her gran!' Sheila insisted. 'Michelle never said any different — how was I to know?'

Sheila moaned all the way through their break about how the girl had played her mistake along and confused things further.

'Most of our mums are in their early twenties. Mind you, I was saying to Kevin that before it's too late we could try again for another baby. He's thinking about it.'

She winked at Jen, who could only wonder if the two of them ever communicated what they were truly thinking to each other.

'We should have made certain we knew who she was.'

Jen was annoyed with Sheila, but had to admit that she herself was so tied up with her personal life, her split, the move and then the events which had happened in the last week, that she had relied on Sheila too much.

'Well, we know now and we'll just have to be careful about what we say around Michelle. She's very observant.'

⋆　⋆　⋆

By the time Jen returned home, she was ready to start anew with her brand new glass door in place.

Aidan's light was off in the upstairs apartment, and her phone rang almost the minute she sat down. She knew the number but also knew it was time to finish this sorry affair — literally — once and for all.

'Jen, babe, where have you been all weekend? I've been so worried about you!'

Harris's voice was unusually soft, gentle even, but she hated it when Harris called her babe. She had to tell him one final time that enough was enough, and that she knew his past was not what he'd revealed to her. She couldn't trust a habitual liar.

'Jen, I want to tell you the truth. All of it, honest.'

She wondered if he even knew the meaning of the word.

'I've been so ashamed of my past life, that I never could say it to you before, but I owe you that much. I'm so sorry.'

266

Jen was riddled with a sudden wave of guilt. Was he being genuine? Perhaps she had acted selfishly? She was so confused by everything that had happened in the last whirlwind couple of days that she didn't know what she felt anymore.

'Well, I had to organise a new back door to be fitted pronto and I've had a lot to sort out regarding the missing stuff. Harris, I want you to understand, that no matter what you feel for me now, well, the truth is I no longer feel that way about you.'

Jen looked around at her plain wall, 'Irish linen' the chart had said. It was definitely plain, like the carpet and the blinds, but the place was fresh. Yet now it was she who felt plain and far from fresh.

She had been so invigorated only a few days earlier, so eager to finish her working week to experience her new life — a new space, a new start — but the break-in had happened and then Harris was here again; she seemed to be slipping back in time. Her linen walls had become as a shroud to her, almost suffocating her, especially when Harris had been there in the midst of her own place surrounded by a total mess.

'Look, Jen, I do understand how you feel. I think I made a bad call. I hid from you what I should have shared, I know that now. I need to see you again and explain. I've been so ashamed, Jen. There were things I wanted to tell you, but I was so scared that if I did I would lose you.' He sniffed. 'Then I did anyway.'

'Honesty is the best policy, Harris,' she said calmly.

Jen knew too well that he had a way of making her feel guilty. Was he going to come clean? Did he really want to change? Was he really crying or welling up with emotion? His voice was breaking as he stuttered his words out. Harris was strong; he didn't behave like that. What had she done to him?

'I could have done all those things for you — the door and all. I know people in the business, but I had to get out of your flat when I did because the cops, they don't forget. They look at records and don't see the person, but you do. You know me, Jen. When I was younger I did time after I was thrown out of the forces. I fell in with the wrong people and was angry, but I'm straight now, honest. The army had helped me and then it felt like I'd been betrayed. I could have gone back to my old ways, but I didn't. I help people at the gym; you've seen the teenagers that come in there when they've nowhere else to go. I give them purpose and set them goals. They learn self respect. You taught me all that, Jen.' He sniffed again.

'Yes I know, but you should have told me the truth before.' Jen was trying not to fall for his silken words.

'I would have lost you sooner if I'd told you all. I'd have scared you off. I wanted you to see me as I am now, so you'd give me a chance . . . ' His voice trailed off and she swallowed, remembering Aidan's warning to her, but he dealt with hard facts and records and she'd known a decent Harris, at least at first.

'Please let me come around and talk to you, or you come down to the gym and talk this through properly. Just one last time, please? Didn't I mean anything to you at all? You meant everything to me.' His voice broke on the last word.

Jen could feel her heart starting to beat to a faster rhythm. She was so confused.

'It won't do any good, Harris. It would only start the hurt again. I wish you well, but I need to make my own life now.'

'Jen, I promise that if you agree to this and I can't convince you that what I say is right, then I'll never bother you ever again. My word on it — one last chance to talk. Or we could do dinner; The Ship is on the corner of your road. One last time . . . please?'

His voice perked up as if he had just remembered. 'Besides you forgot your Kindle.'

Jen knew she had. She'd missed her eBook reader, but didn't want him inside her apartment with the excuse of returning it. She couldn't eat with him there; she was so churned up inside.

'I'll pop by the cafe in half an hour and collect it, but I'm not staying, and Harris, don't even think of making a scene.'

'No way. I just want to explain. I owe you that,' he said, and rang off.

Jen changed into her jeans and trainers and pulled on a loose sweatshirt. She was not dressing up for him; this had to be seen as a casual and fleeting meeting.

She would listen to his lies one last time — even if they were the truth, his words had come too late. Jen simply wanted to collect her Kindle and make it clear that this was the end. No more pestering her incessantly through Sheila, Kevin or gifts of flowers. Her idea of meeting in the café above the gym was, she thought, inspired. It was neutral, visible and would be closing within the hour so he would have to let her go on her way.

★ ★ ★

Jen pulled into an empty parking space on the promenade outside the building which housed the gym, café and salon. Before leaving her Mini and stepping inside the café she sent a quick text to Aidan, as she'd promised she would keep him informed, even though she knew he wouldn't approve of this meeting.

Hi. Had to see Harris to collect my Kindle. Only at Carole's Café. Won't be long and won't take any nonsense. Be back home within the hour. Jen.

She stepped inside the café to see that Harris was already there, sitting at a corner table. He had ordered two cokes and a couple of slices of her favourite lemon drizzle cake. They had the place to themselves, other than the girl at the counter who was busy putting things neatly away.

Good, Jen thought, they wouldn't have long to talk as the place was being made ready to close for the day.

'You won't butter me up with this, you know.' She was amazed that she could even attempt an effort at light humour. Her Kindle had been placed at the side of her plate. She slipped it inside her bag. 'Thanks for that,' she added.

'You know, Jen, you could have let me sort out that place of yours while you moved your stuff back home. A three bedroom house is a lonely place for one person on their ownsome.'

He spoke with what she had once taken as a note of sincerity in his tone, which at one time would have had her heart tugging every which way. Now, seeing his eyes, she realised that it was insincere; it just sounded purely selfish.

'You don't have to sell it,' he went on. 'Flats are very good for the rental market. I know someone who wants one. I'll give him a call if you like. Leave it to me, that's all you have to do.

You believed in me not that long ago, why not now? Just tell me what you paid on it and I'll make sure he pays over, to cover expenses and turn you a profit. They can pay off the mortgage while we — '

'It was a bit crowded in your house when three were in it.' Her remark sounded cold and embittered, even to her ears.

'Jen, please! You know what happened, I explained it to you before but you wouldn't listen. It was Greg's leaving do. How could I know that his sister Kylie had the hots for me? I had a few too many, you know how it is, we were just having fun. My guard was down and I wasn't thinking straight. I just thought if I could get her away from the party, then I could talk to her and sort it out without, you know, embarrassing the lass. Let her down gently, so to speak. I didn't realise it would lead to more trouble, especially between us, Jen. I love you . . . '

Jen remained silent and looked

around. The serving girl was putting her jacket on and they were alone except for her. Jen wondered what had happened to her plan of being in a public place with him as opposed to an isolated one.

'I'll just pop to the bank H,' the girl said. 'Here's the keys. Lock up if you leave before I'm back,' she spoke as she made her way out of the café, leaving only the two of them, and flipped the Open sign to Closed as she went out.

'See, she trusts me,' he said, and shrugged his shoulders.

Jen remained untouched by his words. His admission of love, which she had waited to hear for so long now left her cold, as did the realisation that she was now in the place with just him and he held the keys. How smoothly did that happen?

Harris seemed to realise Jen was not going to respond to his comment and continued, 'It all went wrong. Kylie just stripped off, right in front of me in the lounge. What was I supposed to do?

Throw her out in the street? Come on, Jen, stuff happens; it meant nothing. It's you I want to have kids with, not the likes of her . . . ' He let his voice trail off this time.

'It went very wrong, didn't it, Harris? In fact, if I hadn't forgotten my phone, I wouldn't have come back until much later and then I wouldn't have known anything about it, would I, Harris?' Jen kept her voice calm, sarcasm evident. 'Then the 'stuff' could have gone unnoticed and perhaps happen again.'

He sighed. 'But nothing happened, my word, Jen.'

He stroked the back of her hand with his finger as she rested it on the table.

Jen had a sudden thought, her mind feeling strangely confused, and she said abruptly, 'And just exactly when did we discuss having children? I don't want any for years yet, thanks all the same.'

She saw how dark it was outside and sitting in the café on her own with him, she realised she felt very uneasy; this was not right. It was starting to feel like a trap and she had walked right into it. Well, she would finish up and walk right back out again. She took another sip of her drink.

'Tick-tock, Jen. Biological clock. Better to have them when you're young, or as near to young as you are now.'

Jen looked up. 'Thanks!'

'You know what I mean. It'll only get worse once you tip over thirty and we won't just want to have one, will we?' He added before downing his coke in one and scoffing down the cake. His arms were folded casually on the table as he watched her take her time over her drink.

'I don't want children, not yet, and there is no 'we' anyway,' Jen's voice was sharp. She took another gulp of her drink, put it on the table and turned away from him, but his hand took hold of hers as she had leaned on the table before trying to stand.

He was her ex and he would have to

accept that, which meant all conversations about children with him were irrelevant. His time had gone — *tick-tock* she thought.

Jen stared at the hand holding hers. Gosh, she was tired again. Yet she'd had more sleep in the last three nights than in the previous four added together. She stared at the plates on the table and tried to focus on them. Something was wrong.

She'd spent her lunch time finalising all the form filling that was necessary for the insurance and checking her statement, for what that was worth. She now was the proud owner of a new back door and several locks had appeared on her side gate, courtesy of Mr Marshall, although he did share the passage way between his house and the flats, so there was a little self-interest in his neighbourly gesture. However, she was grateful to be living next to someone who cared about such things.

Yet right now, here, with Harris holding onto her, her ability to focus on where she was and what was happening to her, felt as though it was slipping away from her, beyond her control.

'You're mine, Jen. Don't fight it. You still will be, one last time. You know you want to be, like Kylie did.'

Jen saw Harris move around the table and place an arm around her waist. 'Here, finish your drink. Don't waste it.'

She could feel the liquid being gently poured into her mouth, yet she could not seem to push him away, deny him. She was sinking, the drink . . . she realised as she sunk to her knees and he propped her up against the wall . . . the drink was drugged . . .

Fool!

12

Aidan was in his office when a message registered on his phone. He was aware of it arriving, but had to finish an interview before he could respond. Then he would knock off after what had turned out to be a very long shift.

When he saw who it was from he smiled, until he read her words: *Hi. Had to see Harris to collect my Kindle. Only at Carole's Café. Won't be long and won't take any nonsense. Be back home within the hour. Jen.*

Aidan saw the danger immediately and acted straight away. Leaving word with one of his colleagues where he was going he left his office without delay.

Pulling up outside the café, he cut his lights as he approached. The place was closed up and in the dark. He'd passed the apartment block on his way there and her car was outside, but her apartment was in the dark. Thinking she must have walked there, he'd driven straight to the café.

* * *

Harris grinned. He would now lock up as he had agreed, giving Megan an early finish, as he had paid her to do, knowing trade was always dead at this hour of the day. It was their little secret as he'd explained that he had a special date coming in.

They were all putty in his hands and so easily charmed by him, except Jen it seemed. As he glanced down at Jen, who had slipped to a foetal position on the floor, he thought of how she had offered more of a challenge and although he'd caught her, keeping her had proved to be a bigger problem than he'd envisaged.

That would change. They were going to be together, one last time, as he had promised her. First, though, he had things to do.

Harris rifled through her bag and found her car keys. He'd realised when it was outside the B&B that her car was like a beacon to anyone who knew her. So he saw to closing up the place properly and seeing to Jen, so he could leave her snoozing blissfully in her doped state and, with gloved hands, he drove her Mini back to her apartment and left it there.

He then scaled the iron fence opposite and cut across the closed park, climbing over the bowling hut, to make his quick return via the railway bridge from where it was a clear five minute run through the back streets to the gym and café.

It was just like the old days, he thought, grinning to himself, only with no kit to carry.

His smile dropped, however, when he saw the police car pull up outside the gym, lights off, and the guy from Jen's apartment get out. The sergeant had obviously made his way straight for the café, which was all closed up.

Damn! thought Harris. Was he looking for Jen? Surely not. How the hell did he know where she was? Unless of course the two-timing bitch had told him where she was going? Were they joined at the hip already? Clearly Jen didn't trust him at all, and that hurt.

Harris ran down a back alley, taking a few quick turns to wend his way to the rear of the building. He climbed into the back of the gym through the old cellar hatch. He always left it open during the hours he was there, just in case there was any trouble, like the uniformed kind who lurked outside. It always paid to have an escape route planned.

As he entered the building he pulled off his leather gloves and tossed them onto a chair and nodded to a couple of his regulars. He cast his sweater off revealing a muscular frame in a T-Back black vest.

When the door opened and Sergeant Lee walked in, Harris was busy talking about weights, seemingly deep in conversation and instruction.

'Dalton,' Aidan said without pre-amble, and continued to walk into the gym. He went straight to the door and glanced into the empty back room.

'You looking for me? 'Cos if you are, I'm stood right here!' Harris snapped, as if he was offended by the sergeant's high-handedness.

'Where is Miss Brightman?' Lee demanded.

'She left,' Harris decided that he obviously knew they'd met, so there was no use denying it. 'Why? She in trouble again?'

'When?' The sergeant seemed to ignore his question.

Harris looked back at the man he'd been talking to.

'Well, I'm not sure but I've been back here about twenty or twenty-five min-utes.' His friend nodded as if that sounded a reasonable estimation. 'So she must have left just before that, when the café was closed up. Why?' he asked as innocently as he could, but with a more determined tone to his voice.

'She's not answering her phone she's not at home.' Lee looked around seemingly taking in every detail.

'That's women for you — fickle!'

Harris looked at the man who was working out and returned to instructing him about his breathing. The other man grinned.

The sergeant did not. 'I want to see inside the café,' he demanded firmly.

Harris didn't turn back around to look at the man, but answered casually as if he was being rational and patient with the disturbance to his work. Harris was impressed by his own ability to be cool.

'I've got Carole's number some-where, but she won't be happy about you dragging her back here at this time 'cos she's going out with her fiancé tonight — special occasion.'

'She won't have to; she already told me you have a key for emergency use, as does the salon owner and vice-versa.'

Harris almost grinned at the man's determination. He'd obviously been busy on his phone, this upstart. He was arrogant, though, if he thought he could outwit Harris G Dalton.

'Well, if you have her permission. I'll just phone and check.' Harris enjoyed playing this game of good citizen.

'I already did, which is why I know you all have a set to each other's businesses.'

'Very well,' he turned to the few club members that were in, 'Won't be a minute, lads.'

Harris collected a bunch of keys from his desk and walked out, not even looking back at the copper. He'd noted his name and face and Harris was sure he could arrange to have it rearranged sometime in the next few weeks. Col, his friend from a local karate dojo, owed him a favour, big time.

Harris smiled at the sergeant — how he hated uniforms now — and politely said, 'After you.'

The man just glared at him, and it

was then that Harris realised that there was more to this man's interest than professional concern. He looked into the man's eyes and could sense that he was genuinely worried about Jen; she had got herself a new admirer.

Harris walked out into the night and approached the café door from the street level. He wondered if this pup of a copper was the reason why his Jen wouldn't come back to him. The copper had obviously told her of his past otherwise she wouldn't be aware of it. Certainly Kevin didn't know, so Sheila had no notion of it either. And the copper had been quite comfortable standing in Jen's bedroom, with her finery on display.

Harris unlocked the café door and stepped back.

The sergeant did not move in, but waited for him to go first. He flicked the lights on and stepped inside, smug, arms folded.

The tables were stacked with the chairs atop like a school room after home time.

There was no sign of anyone there. Everything had been washed, shut down and replaced ready for another day.

'What's through there?' Aidan Lee asked.

'The store room, supplies and staff room of sorts,' Harris said and stifled a yawn.

Aidan gestured that they should go further inside, which they did. He had Harris open the cleaning cupboard door, the toilet door — still nothing. Harris could feel the tension in the man; he had really got it bad for her. It amused him to think that the woman who had been taken in by a conman had managed to dupe a copper.

'You said she left here, with her iPad?' Aidan Lee asked.

'No, I didn't. I just said that she left here — and it was her Kindle that she collected from me, constable,' he chided. The man ignored his comment.

'Don't go far. I'll be back.' Lee walked out into the street.

Harris almost laughed at the guy's obvious frustration, but he knew better than to get too cocky in front of him. Realising that time was going by and he'd not been planning for Jen to just enjoy a good sleep, he had no alternative but to lock up and return to the gym until he was sure the copper had gone.

★　★　★

Aidan tried the apartment again and soon realised that Jen had not returned, but the car was still there, which was odd. He looked up at his own apartment and sighed.

Then he realised his mistake and cringed at his own stupidity. They each had a set of keys to the businesses in the building — not two, but three. Harris had access to the hairdresser's salon on the second floor, too.

★　★　★

Harris had intended to go straight back to Jen, but time had passed by. He picked up another bottle of coke and one of his 'special pills' from the drawer. He had never used a double-dose before, but if the drug started to show signs of lifting he just might, either way, better to be prepared.

He unlocked the salon door and walked into the main room, straight past the hairdressing stations to the beauty room at the end. Sliding the door back, he saw Jen — his Jen, not some copper's — lying on the bench where he'd left her. He had cocooned her in the blanket as the beauticians did. It had been like settling a baby in a papoose.

She had stayed in a half-asleep, half-awake slumber all nicely wrapped up for him, all comfortable and warm and now, as he looked at her eagerly, he intended to unwrap his present.

He slid the door closed and lit the candles which they used to calm and scent the air. He breathed in the aromas and even Harris had to admit that they were far more pleasant than the ones that permeated the gym. But that was a man's world and this was a feminine place.

He slipped his Smartphone out of his pocket and left it on the counter at the side ready to capture the image of beauty he wanted to own. He would have a lasting record of his girl, before she walked for good. He'd already decided that she would wake in his bed and not know what had happened, then he would tell her that they had made up.

Jen's head had turned toward the light source. Those heavy-lidded blue-green eyes stared at the flickering flames of the candles; the same flame which highlighted the colours of her hair. Harris slowly unwrapped the blanket and looked at her. He was not a sentimental man but she was, to him, the epitome of perfection. Not the plastic artificial type, that could be bought, but the natural athletic sort that could only be earned.

He gently slipped off her boots and

his hands stroked her legs as he made for the button at the top of her jeans. She was hardly aware of the zip sliding down as he then pulled the fabric firmly along the length of her legs.

'My beauty,' he whispered as he discarded her jeans with the boots. Her head flopped one way and then the other and he suspected that deep down she was trying to pull herself back up to a more conscious state, but as the palm of his hand stroked the flat of her abdomen slowly, she settled again.

Next he lifted the edge of her top. He smiled at the laciest of bras underneath, which matched her pants perfectly.

'Such class,' he said. He held her to him with one strong arm as he reached out for his phone with his free hand. It would be the best shoot yet. She would put the others to shame, including the latest one. That one was Jen's fault, because she had made him so angry.

'Come here my beauty,' he said. 'Smile at the birdy . . . '

He tried to take a shot of her with the

phone's camera but she was draped on him and he could not get the angle right. He put his phone down and decided he would have to try again in a moment and smiled broadly.

'Now, my treasure, will you show me how sorry you are for hurting Harris?'

Harris heard nothing, but felt the strike as he was knocked to the ground with one head-reeling punch.

It was so unexpected that he was on the floor before his senses had recovered enough to respond and by then it was too late. His hands were cuffed and two coppers dragged him to his feet and bundled him out into the now fully-lit salon, where he was cautioned on the spot.

'Take him in. I'll stay here until the medics arrive for Miss Brightman,' Aidan Lee instricted from where he stood inside the small room, where Jen was trying to stand up and nearly falling off the beautician's spa couch.

Aidan acted quickly, propping her up and looked into her eyes, seeing that she was still under the influence of the drugs. He saw the phone lying on the counter and, knowing what he was about to do was wrong, he flicked through the gallery and saw images of the other poor girl that Harris had doped. Aidan saw that there were plenty of images stored to get Harris sent down, including the latest victim from last weekend.

Fortunately there were none of Jen and he quickly helped her back into her top and jeans.

'You really are too trusting, Jen,' he muttered to her, but the answer he received was incoherent and he reluctantly left her with the paramedics to be taken in for a check up.

The phone, a pill and the bottle of coke were retrieved from the counter. Before the evening was out, more pills had been recovered from the gym.

Both Harris and his partner had a different business going on, peddling substances to members and supplying runners, the teenagers they were helping to a so-called better life.

With Jen safe, and Dalton at last locked up where he deserved to be and with the evidence filed and statements taken — except Jen's; that would have to wait a few more hours and he knew it would be vague beyond sipping her drink — all was done that could be done.

★ ★ ★

The next morning Aidan turned his attention to the gifts that had been sent to Jen and the mysterious phone messages.

The phone number was registered to a man who turned out to have died the previous summer. Yet the phone had been continuously topped up and used. No clear lead there.

The bottle had Bill's prints on it and Jen's — no-one else's. The chocolates had been disposed of and the petals had never been seen by him and they too had gone. The gift cards were equally unhelpful. Somehow, somewhere, there was menace in all of these events, but he was missing a vital connection.

Aidan played with his phone and, as he drank a cup of tea in his apartment, he dialled the number of the dead caller again.

This time it rang. He placed his mug down on the counter top and waited, longing for someone to answer it. It rang and rang and then stopped. This time it was not switched off.

'Hello, who's there?' Aidan asked gently. 'I want to help you. Please answer me. Is this Mr Johnson?' Aidan asked for the man whose phone it had been, hoping this would illicit some kind of response.

'No.'

The one word reply made Aidan sit up. He'd not expected what sounded like the voice of a child to be at the other end. The gifts had certainly not been sent by any child, surely?

'Oh dear, I seem to have phoned the wrong person. What's your name?'

Aidan tried to sound friendly. If he said he was a policeman the child might switch it off, frightened rather than reassured. 'Is this your phone?' he persisted.

'I found it,' the girl's voice replied. 'I didn't steal it.'

Aidan smiled. 'You are a clever girl. I'm a policeman and we've been looking for this phone. Tell me what's your name and where you found it? We couldn't find it even though we were looking for it, so you're very clever.'

'I found it in the bin. Miss threw it away. It's got a low battery. I'm Michelle and — Mummy!'

Aidan heard the words; he was instantly hit by a thought that he just as quickly dismissed. If this was a child from Jen's school, surely Jen had not sent the gifts and the messages to herself! He knew of such cases where people sought attention, but not Jen, she was too grounded. He just knew there had to be another explanation.

'Who is this speaking?' an angry

adult voice demanded.

'I'm Sergeant Lee. Please don't hang up. We needed to trace this phone.'

'I don't know whose phone this is. My daughter says she found it . . . '

'Please tell me where you are and I'll come over and explain. I really am a policeman and your daughter deserves a reward for recovering this mobile. It's a vital piece of evidence.'

13

Jen returned home, cleared of any ill effects and still buzzing with the shame of it all. She had given her statement, as much as she could remember about going to the café, to the PC who had come to visit her.

She'd seen no sign of Aidan and she strongly suspected that he was disgusted with her for running back to Harris, at least that must be what it looked like to him.

As for her own feelings of revulsion that she had been so completely duped by the man, she would need time to come to terms with that.

Jen hadn't had any calls from Sheila either. Mr Marshall had left a note to say that if she needed anything she was to phone him, but everyone seemed to be staying well away from her.

How would she face school again?

Then she realised that when Sheila found out about Harris, she would be distraught, as she'd also been completely taken in by the man. She felt somehow tainted. Her new found addiction seemed to be cleaning her flat, bathing and trying to reduce the detritus that she felt clung to her. Being active made her feel less down about all these recent events.

She was deeply in thought, trying to blot any memory of Harris from her mind, when the doorbell rang and she jumped up, snapping back to reality.

If this was Sheila visiting then she'd tell her that they had both been fools.

However, the thought of facing her made Jen's stomach flip with anxiety and the trauma she still felt after having so nearly been . . . she shuddered at the thought.

When she opened the door and saw the tall figure standing at the other side of her frosted glass pane she felt relieved. Her mood improved instantly and her confidence was restored on recognising the outline of Aidan Lee standing there.

'Hello . . . Come in,' she said awkwardly. He smiled at her, but his eyes betrayed the troubled nature of his visit.

'How are you?' he asked as he entered.

'I'm getting there.' She closed the door and locked it. 'I don't know where to even begin to apologise for my own stupidity — or thank you for coming to my rescue.' She forced herself to meet his eyes, feeling so ashamed. 'I understand that you found me with him and that he was . . . '

Aidan gently pulled her into him in a natural gesture, putting a protective arm around her as her tears welled up.

'I got there before there was any real harm done.'

'The constable told me he had pictures of girls on his phone and I wondered if . . . '

'No, there were none of you. I arrived there in time to stop him. You were asleep, that's all.'

She nodded and felt flushed with relief.

'Jen, you'd better come in and sit down. I have to tell you something and it won't be an easy thing for you to take in.'

Jen followed him into her own room, led by the hand as if she were a child, and sat down as she was told to.

'The messages came from a mobile that belonged to the sender's father-in-law. He died last summer, so they pocketed the phone and used it as a spare. When you were burgled, and when I turned up and a thorough investigation began, things became more complicated for this person's plans. They decided to lose the phone in the school's bin.'

He paused, waiting for the information to sink in before he went on. 'That was their mistake because you have in your class a very bright young lady who thought that even if the phone was broken the games might still work. She had even figured out that if there was no battery life, she could give it to the charity people for recycling.'

'Michelle?' Jen said, and then added, 'Of course. I always felt as if she knew something.'

Aidan nodded.

'Who was it? Kevin? He came to the school and . . . '

Jen was holding Aidan's hand without realising it.

His look told her that the truth would be more surprising than his revelations to date.

'Mr Finch? Surely not?'

'Sheila had seen Kevin make a pass at you last Christmas and you cut him dead. She also saw you turn Harris down, someone she had admired for years. You bought a new car, a new apartment, you have a salary far exceeding hers. You were planning a summer holiday in Hong Kong and she had a week in Skegness for the family,' Aidan explained.

Jen simply sat and listened, barely able to comprehend.

'You refused to balance the little

foursome again and be with her as her friend in her world,' he went on. 'You escaped it and she couldn't. She thought you'd betrayed her and she wanted to break your confidence and drive you back to Harris.'

'Sheila was jealous of me? To the extent that she wanted to harm me?'

Jen gripped her own sides as if she were trying to hug herself, to defend herself against this devastating news. She had confided in the one person that she trusted, closest to her in her work and her world.

'No, not physically.'

'But the wine . . . ?'

'That was delivered and tampered with by Kevin. Sheila denies poisoning it. It was that accusation that broke her resolve not to admit to anything. And once she heard about the drugs, and she realised where Kevin's extra cash had come from then she crumpled and told us everything.'

'What will happen to her? What about the children?'

'She needs help, but not from you. You let the authorities handle this. What Kevin and Harris have been doing will see them go down. This is beyond your control now and you need to focus on yourself.'

'Should I speak to her?' Jen asked, numbed by the news.

'No, I would leave things be, Jen. She thought, in her strange disturbed logic, that if you were driven back to Harris, then things would be as they were again. She didn't know Harris was a dealer or that you'd be targeted by a burglar. Ironically, he was one of Harris's customers.'

Jen leaned into Aidan, her mind swirling with all this information. She couldn't believe that she'd been so easily taken in. But at last it was all over.

Her life had just changed forever, but now she would be free of them all and that new start that she had so longed for all these weeks would finally begin.

* * *

Jen stayed in Aidan's apartment that night and all of the next week, too. She eventually moved back in to her own flat when all the gossip and fury had died down at work and the legalities had finally been dealt with.

Planning to resign in the following July, Jen had already handed in her notice. When she did she felt a weight lift from her shoulders and, after it was done, she couldn't wait to tell Aidan. She needed to know he had not changed his mind either.

She was already thinking of moving on — again.

Flats were going fast in the area so it was possible, if she could push up the price to cover yet another sale, then she would sell up. Jen wanted to learn from her mistake and start again, even if that meant leaving the area.

*   *   *

As soon as she had entered Aidan's apartment later that day, she blurted out her news straight away.

'I did it! I've resigned!'

'That's great!'

Aidan was dressed casually in jeans and a fine blue-stripe shirt, and he smiled as he put dinner on the table.

'Then let's make those bookings and you can accept your new teaching post from September.'

Jen hugged him closely and felt so happy — so loved and appreciated — that everything that had happened in the last few months now seemed so blissfully distant.

'Are you sure?'

'Jen!' He looked at the ceiling, rolling his eyes, but with mirth in them, too.

'I wouldn't have offered to be your guide to Hong Kong if I wasn't sure,' he told her. 'But remember, there's no pressure. Like I said, I'm here for you and we can just be friends for as long as you need. You have to learn to live again without constantly looking over your shoulder. We'll have a great time, you'll see, and if something else develops over time, well, we'll just take it slow, one step at a time.'

Jen smiled at him and looked longingly at the food in front of her; Aidan cooking for her was just one of the many ways he made her feel special.

Picking up her glass of wine — Merlot, of course — she raised it high and said happily, 'To freedom!'

Aidan smiled back, raised his cup of jasmine tea and replied, 'To freedom — and to us!'

THE END

CHLOE'S FRIEND
A PHOENIX RISES
ABIGAIL MOOR:
THE DARKEST DAWN
DISCOVERING ELLIE
TRUTH, LOVE AND LIES
SOPHIE'S DREAM

We do hope that you have enjoyed reading this large print book.

Did you know that all of our titles are available for purchase?

We publish a wide range of high quality large print books including:
Romances, Mysteries, Classics
General Fiction
Non Fiction and Westerns

Special interest titles available in large print are:
The Little Oxford Dictionary
Music Book, Song Book
Hymn Book, Service Book

Also available from us courtesy of Oxford University Press:
Young Readers' Dictionary
(large print edition)
Young Readers' Thesaurus
(large print edition)

For further information or a free brochure, please contact us at:
Ulverscroft Large Print Books Ltd.,
The Green, Bradgate Road, Anstey,
Leicester, LE7 7FU, England.
Tel: (00 44) **0116 236 4325**
Fax: (00 44) **0116 234 0205**

Other titles in the
Linford Romance Library:

SINISTER ISLE OF LOVE

Phyllis Mallett

Jenny Carr is joining her brother on the Caribbean island of Taminga to start a new life. On her way, she meets Peter Blaine, a successful businessman on the island. He couldn't be more of a contrast to Craig Hannant, whose business is failing. His wife had died in mysterious circumstances, and Craig is now a difficult man to be around — but Jenny falls for Craig, despite all the signs that she is making the biggest mistake of her life . . .

CUPID'S BOW

Toni Anders

When romantic novelist Janey first meets Ashe Corby, she is not impressed. But frustratingly, the hero in the latest novel she is writing persists in resembling him! As Janey gets to know Ashe, she comes to admire and like him. But when she attempts to help Ashe's son Daniel to realise his dream of studying horticulture, Ashe is furious at what he sees as interference on Janey's part. Miserable without each other, will love win through for them?

MISTLETOE MEDICINE

Anna Ramsay

Ever since he wrecked her romance with Dickie Derby, Nurse Hannah Westcott has harboured a thorough dislike of Dr Jonathan Boyd-Harrington — but she never expected to see him again. To her horror, he turns up as Senior Registrar at the Royal Hanoverian Hospital, and there is no way she can avoid him — especially when he takes an interest in the hospital panto. Hannah has the star part, but it would seem she must play Nurse Beauty to Jonathan Boyd-Harrington's Dr Beast . . .